She opened the door.

Beyond, it was dark, a night sky, yet flooded with an eerie incandescent light that she realised after a moment was moonlight. Moonlight lit up and bisected with hard shadows a long street, colonnaded on both sides. Its pale gleam outlined carved pillars, ornate doorways, stone faces grimacing at her. The road was paved with cobbles, sharply contoured by shadow. The stonework was dark bronze in colour, as though shot through with ore. At the end of the street was a high tower, coiling upwards from its base to finish in an elegant spindle of lacy stone and metalwork.

All windows were shuttered, there was not a soul to be seen, though a dog barked somewhere in the distance. A pillar had fallen, and lay cracked across the street, and some of the stonework had crumbled away.

CITYSCAPE

FRANCES THOMAS

Teens · Mandarin

First published in Great Britain 1988
by William Heinemann Ltd
Published 1990 by Teens · Mandarin
an imprint of Mandarin Paperbacks
Michelin House, 81 Fulham Road, London SW3 6RB

Mandarin is an imprint of the Octopus Publishing Group

Copyright © 1988 Frances Thomas

ISBN 0 7497 0206 0

A CIP catalogue record for this title
is available from the British Library

Printed in Great Britain
by Cox & Wyman Ltd, Reading, Berkshire

Now you see it, now you don't.

The door was there, and then it was not there.

It had been there that morning, in the subway at Shepherds Bush: an ordinary door of indeterminate colour set into the wall of ribbed and darkly glittering tiles. As she approached it, it seemed to shimmer, as though unsure of its existence. Then a drunken tramp whom she had not noticed before rallied himself from a pile of dirty clothing, and began to shout at her. She pulled her dignity about her like a cloak, and hurried on and out of the subway, into the sodden greyness of a November morning.

In the evening, coming home from school, she took the subway again. The tramp was no longer there, and neither was the door.

On Thursday evening, she came home the long way, through Holland Park. There had been a Jacobean mansion here, before it was bombed in the war, and you could still see the ghost of it, a wing of rosy brick, with undulating parapet, steps that led into emptiness, doors that went nowhere, paths that began and did not finish. The gardens were still there, a formality of fountains and lavender hedges, arbours and terraces, lawns where peacocks walked. She liked to imagine herself mistress of such a place, gliding through passages, clipping faded roses into a basket.

She saw herself now, pushing open the door that was set into the wall here below twisted thick creeper stems, into who knows what secret garden beyond!

But she was no gracious chatelaine. She was only Debra Stoner, fifteen and fat, her assets for the moment, at any rate, hidden. (A good brain was the chief of them, but that came quite low down the scale of virtues admired at her school.) And she was cold. She went to the coffee shop and bought herself some coffee in a polystyrene cup, and cradled it in her hands, as she retraced her steps down the walled walk.

Towards the door.

Which was not now there.

And it wasn't just appearing and disappearing doors that made her feel that half of her was not quite anchored in reality; there was the dream as well. She had had recurring dreams before, but never one like this, with the precision of real memory.

A dusty ballroom; sunlight shafting through the air, everything pale and faded. At a table sat a man: she assumed it must be a man, though she could only make out a hunched outline. He was writing, slowly, meticulously, holding his pen awkwardly.

An empty ornate room. A man writing. Who was he, and what did he write so carefully?

Ever since her mother had gone back to Ireland, she'd had the dream regularly. So regularly now that it fitted seamlessly into the fabric of her ordinary life.

She threw the rest of her coffee away, and hurried off homewards. It was not quite dark, though not quite light

2

either. Mist swallowed up the distances in the park, and reduced everything to monotone, except for here and there the vivid moving dots of tracksuited joggers. London was grey on grey on grey. Traffic spun threads of gold light in the gloom; cars hissed on the damp surface.

The other day when their geography teacher had not turned up, another teacher, filling in, gave them a general knowledge quiz. The class divided into Team A and Team B. The questions seemed to Debra ridiculously simple, and after a couple of correct answers, she held herself back. But if she hoped not to be noticed by this stratagem, she was wrong. Matthew Best in the other team was asked 'What is the world's biggest mammal?' Without a second's hesitation he replied 'Debra Stoner,' and the class erupted into laughter, in which Debra tried, not very successfully, to join.

You see, what you had to be was not clever, and definitely not fat. On top of that, you had to have a hide like a rhinoceros. The more they laughed the harder it got to take. And the more she dug herself into the shell that was the last thing in the world that she wanted to carry around with her.

But how did you get out of it?

Miss Lovelace thought she had the answer. Miss Lovelace thought she had all the answers. She was young, barely out of college, but with that utter self-confidence that Debra half despised, half envied like mad. Moreover, Miss Lovelace fancied herself as a psychologist. One day, she collared Debra in the corridor, and treated her to five minutes of amateur Freud. 'You see, the trouble with you, Debra, is that you think too much about yourself. Mmn? Self-consciousness, you see, Debra, is simply another form of conceit. Mmn?' Miss Lovelace always finished her sentences on that rising interrogative. And the stupid thing was, she expected you to answer, to concur in the brisk demolition job she was doing on your character. *Yes, Miss Lovelace. I quite agree. I'm a conceited cow. Certainly, Miss Lovelace* . . . And then, pleased with what she had done, Miss Lovelace swanned off, leaving Debra feeling six inches smaller. And half a ton fatter.

Blast Miss Lovelace!

Blast Matthew Best!

Blast the rest of them!

But then you could just see Miss Lovelace getting her sharp little teeth into that one! *Imagining everyone's against you: that's what we call paranoia, Debra. Mmn? You don't want to be a paranoiac now, do you? Mmn?*

Going home, she avoided the subway, risking instead a perilous zig-zag through slow moving traffic, coming in for a good assortment of horn beeping and abuse as she did so. But it was better than disappearing doors, thank you very much.

> *The other day, upon the stair,*
> *I met a door that wasn't there.*
> *It wasn't there again today;*
> *I wish that door would go away!*

Home was the Orchard Estate. Aspen Towers, Oak Towers, Beech Towers. The Towers were blocks of concrete, twenty storeys into the sky; the trees were nowhere to be seen. To get to the Estate, you turned down Pickett's Barn Lane. Perhaps somewhere beneath the concrete, the spirit of Mr Pickett, his orchard and his barn, stirred uneasily, but as Debra hurried through the walkways, and newspapers and chip-papers blew against

4

her legs, and angry graffiti stared at her, there was no sign that anything other than concrete had ever existed here.

Debra and her mother lived on the thirteenth floor. It was the thirteenth floor in fact, though not in name. It was called the fourteenth, but as Debra's mother said, you didn't turn something into something else simply by giving it a different name.

The block was crammed with people, but you seldom saw them, though you could hear the barking of the outsize dogs that many tenants kept illegally to scare off marauders. At least today the lift was working.

Her mother had been trying to get a transfer for years. Debra's father's death, in a car crash ten years before, had left them in a financial mess. When they'd moved to the Orchard Estate, Debra's mother swore it was only a temporary thing. But they were still here. She was on the list for a transfer, but there were far more pressing cases than a widow with a teenage daughter. Meanwhile, Debra's mother continued to dream of a little house in a tree-lined suburb that one day she'd have the keys of.

At the moment, she was in Ireland, where she had been for the last two weeks, coping with the situation left by her sister Mary's illness and death. Mary left two young children, and her husband had walked out on her; things would not be easy. Debra's mother still talked about the wonderful old days in the family home. Mary and Fergus, Billy and Kath and Joe. You would think there'd never been a family like them, with their laughing and their jokes and their affection. Debra grew sick of hearing about them sometimes. She wondered what she would find to tell her own children one day. 'Ah, the times we had dodging the muggers on the Orchard Estate!'

She'd only been to Ireland once, and though they'd all been nice enough and friendly in a vague kind of way, she felt they were all too bound up with one another to let her into the charmed circle. Mum had stopped going to church, too, and while for some reason this didn't seem to exclude her from their number, it had the effect of excluding Debra. Moreover, she didn't look like them. Her own Dad had been half Indian, which meant that she wasn't quite one thing or the other. Either way, she didn't feel that there was anywhere she belonged.

Certainly not the Orchard Estate. She opened the door of her flat, and thankfully went in, bolting and chaining the door behind her. She was locked in now till morning.

She did her homework, read a chapter of *Wuthering Heights* which she was reading for the third time, cooked herself a meal, had too much to eat and felt sick. ('No wonder you're so big, the way you stuff yourself,' said her mother, who weighed seven and a half stone.) When you were on your own, nothing took up very much time. She watched television until midnight, and then went to bed.

In bed, came the dream. The way the man was writing reminded her of a child, he was so hunched and awkward. But she knew that he wasn't a child, and that his writing was of vital importance. In the morning, she woke: a grey sky outside her window, and no explanations.

2

'Debra!'

Coming up the steps behind her was Matthew Best, dressed in old jeans and an expensive leather jacket. His father was rich, and in the film world. There was something the matter with his mother. The rumour varied as to what it was: some people said she was a nut, some an alcoholic. Matthew had only joined the school six months ago, from an expensive boarding school where he claimed to have been unhappy.

'*Debra!*'

'What?'

'I want to talk to you.'

'Well, I don't want to talk to you, thanks very much.'

Steve and Jonesey came past. 'Hi, Mammal,' they called. It was the nickname she'd had since Matthew's little joke. She tried to pretend she hadn't heard, and turned away into the toilets.

In the toilets, Rachel Ward and Sharon Black combed their hair. Rachel was a dazzling blonde.

'So what did you *say*?' giggled Sharon.

'Told him to get lost, didn't I?' said Rachel with a shrug of her beautiful shoulders. 'Oh it's the Mammal. Hi, Mammal.'

'Ooh, you are *mean*!' Sharon sniggered.

* * *

The school was to go on strike. There'd been a rumour going for some time, but at lunch, it was confirmed. Complete closure until the end of the week. After that, it was anyone's guess. Cries of glee went up at the news.

Debra did not know whether she'd be happier in school or out of it. Staying at school to be called The Mammal every five minutes, or at home, to do what? Stare out at the Estate? Roam the streets? No doubt a phone call to Dublin would bring Mum home on the next boat, but . . .

No, she would look after herself.

If it killed her.

Matthew Best was there again, outside the school gates. What the hell did he want?

'What the hell do you want, Matthew Best?'

'I just wanted to talk.'

'You've talked enough, big mouth.'

'Look, I just . . .'

Debra hurried off. She heard him running behind her, so she turned sharply into the Park. November damp hung in the air, and the gravel crunched beneath her shoes. She strode briskly down paths, between trees. She did not look to see if he was still there, but after a while there were no more footsteps.

But she was panting, and she realised just how fast she'd been walking. As though she had been escaping somebody, which was daft, because Matthew certainly wasn't worth the trouble of avoiding. She found she was in a bit of the Park she didn't know well. The path turned sharply, and wound round the back of a building. There was a wheelbarrow, stacked with a few last dead leaves and a rake, resting against a door in the old brick wall.

* * *

Open me, said the door, *I dare you.*

Physically timid, Debra had never been much of a one to respond to dares. The door confronted her, battered and ordinary, wood bleached silvery with age. The handle was a ring of wrought iron. *Go on, turn me.*

She opened the door.

Beyond, it was dark, a night sky, yet flooded with an eerie incandescent light that she realised after a moment was moonlight. Moonlight lit up and bisected with hard shadows a long street, colonnaded on both sides. Its pale gleam outlined carved pillars, ornate doorways, stone faces grimacing at her. The road was paved with cobbles, sharply contoured by shadow. The stonework was dark bronze in colour, as though shot through with ore. At the end of the street was a high tower, coiling upwards from its base to finish in an elegant spindle of lacy stone and metalwork.

All windows were shuttered, there was not a soul to be seen, though a dog barked somewhere in the distance. A pillar had fallen, and lay cracked across the street, and some of the stonework had crumbled away.

She tried to step through into the street, but could not. She stood in a thick, foggy darkness. It was all around her. She turned round, looking for the wheelbarrow and the rake. For a moment, she could not see them, but the mist cleared and there they were frosted with November rain, under a grey sky.

The moonlit street had gone. The door had gone, too.

Now you see it.

Now you don't.

3

He was still there, following her. Why must he follow her everywhere? She went to the library to work, but as she crossed the wide brick path that led to the main door, there he was, popping out from behind a pillar, like a jack-in-the-box.

'Debra, *please*.'

'I don't know what you want.'

'Well, of course you don't, wally, you won't let me say.'

She saw the logic of this. 'What *do* you want to say?'

'That's better.' He caught her up. 'Phew. Want a coffee?'

'I'm broke.'

'I'm not. MacDonalds?'

'If you like.'

He thrust his hands into the pockets of the leather jacket and grinned at her. His short spiky hair looked as though it had been the loser in an argument with a bleach bottle. One of his front teeth was chipped.

'Are you all right, Debra?'

'What do you mean?'

'Well, you look . . .'

'I look what?'

'Worried, I guess.'

What did you say to that? Did you say, of course I'm worried. I've just walked through a door that wasn't there, into a moonlit night in the middle of the day, in a city street in the middle of Holland Park? No, you did not. You smiled, and said 'I'm okay.'

'Great. Hey, it's bad about this strike, isn't it?'

'Is it?'

'You think, phew, no school. Then you think, no school, what the hell am I going to do all day? You're staying on your own, at the moment, aren't you?'

'How do you know?'

'Katie Lane said. What is it, a funeral?'

'My aunt's. In Dublin.'

'I'm on my own too. My dad's away. And my mum. Well, she's away, too. It gets boring after a while.'

Debra shrugged. 'I can look after myself.'

'Oh, we all *can*. The question is, do you like it?'

Debra wrestled with her pride. 'Not a lot, I suppose.'

They came to MacDonalds, and went in. 'What was it you wanted to say to me?'

'Coffee first. Or coke, which would you prefer?'

'Coffee, please. It's too cold for coke.'

She found a table by the window, and watched him while he collected the coffee from the counter, with a grin at the girl who was serving. Meanwhile, Debra began to pull herself together. The more she thought about the thing in the park, the more she thought she could convince herself that it had not really happened. There had been no door, she had not opened a door, she had not looked through. It must all have been some kind of hallucination. That's what it was. A hallucination.

But that started her mind going all over again. For if you had hallucinations it meant you were mad. And surely, whatever else she might be, she wasn't mad.

11

So it wasn't a hallucination. But then again, what was it?

Matthew returned with the coffee. 'There you are, madame. A cup of coffee prepared from finest coffee beans, exclusively blended by a secret process.'

She smiled, in spite of herself. 'Do you always go on like this?'

'Only when I'm with a beautiful girl. I get nervous, you see.' He emptied large amounts of sugar into his cup.

'You'll rot your teeth.'

In reply he grinned at her. 'Hey, did you know, that if you didn't shut your eyes when you sneeze, your eyes would fall out?'

'No, I didn't,' said Debra. 'Thanks.'

'Anything you want to know, just ask.'

'All I want to know is this mysterious thing you want to talk about.'

'Not mysterious, really. I just wanted to apologise.'

'What for?' She knew what for, of course. And oddly, the thought of him apologising was almost unwelcome. It was as though she felt better if she could dislike him.

'You know very well what for.'

'For my charming nickname?'

'Yes. Well, I never realised people would . . . you know . . . pick it up like that.'

She shrugged, unsure how to respond gracefully.

'Still, I *was* mad at you. That's why I said it in the first place.'

'Mad at *me*?'

'What you said. Don't you remember?'

'No.'

'What, you really can't remember what you said to me the day before?'

'No, I can't.'

'Bloody hell.'

'Matthew, tell me. What did I say?'

'You honestly can't remember?'

'I told you.'

'Well, the day before, I'd asked you, who wrote *Wuthering Heights*, was it Jane Austen?'

'So. What did I say?' But Debra began dimly to remember.

'The exact words, I believe, were, *If you think that, Matthew Best, then you're even more stupid than you look.*'

'Yes, but . . .'

'Yes, but?'

'I didn't *mean* that, wally. It was just something to say.'

'I was furious with you.'

'I'm sorry. But honestly, I didn't mean to upset you.'

'I didn't mean to upset *you*.'

'I didn't say it to you in front of the entire class.'

'Maybe not, but you just got up my nose.'

Debra started to protest, but he silenced her. 'Shall we call it quits, then?'

'I suppose so,' she began less than graciously, but changed her mind and grinned. 'Yeah. Okay. Why not?'

'Phew,' he said, wiping his brow exaggeratedly. 'That was a close shave.' Suddenly he leaned forward and took her hand. 'Hasn't anyone ever told you, my dear,' he said in Cary Grant tones, 'that you're beautiful when you smile?'

'Has anyone ever told you,' she said, 'that you're daft?'

'Yeah, but it's better than being sensible, isn't it?'

'Is it?'

'It certainly is,' he said. 'Being sensible gets you precisely nowhere in this world, or so I've noticed. So are we friends now, Debra, or what?'

She thought about it. There seemed little reason to go on being angry now. 'Yes, I suppose so, if you want.'

To her surprise, he looked pleased. A big grin lit up his face, and he drank down the rest of his coffee with a gulp, as though to distract attention from himself. 'Listen, if this stupid strike's still on tomorrow, shall I meet you?'

'Yes, all right. Why not?'

She walked home through an afternoon that was fast turning to evening. In the large houses on Holland Park, lamps were being lit, and heavy curtains drawn. She wondered about all the lives that went on behind those elegant windows, and though somebody – her mother most probably – popped up in her thoughts to tell her that she should not go envying other people their lives (you just don't know what it is you think you're envying, my girl), she could not help it tonight, when she remembered the empty flat and a frozen meal awaiting her.

The Estate was quiet tonight, quiet and cold. The great blocks rose weightlessly out of the gloom, as though they were afloat in the chill November mist, like hulks moored on a river. The smell of winter was in the air, sucked in by the winds that always blew round here. She saw no-one as she crossed the forecourt, but their names stared at her in jagged graffiti – Ray, Chaz, The King.

There was no-one in the lift either, and it whirred her up to her floor silently enough. Its dingy grey walls, its eerie silence, always made her feel that she was taking a journey to somewhere lost and unpleasant, a sort of Hades in the sky perhaps. But it disgorged her as usual on the corridor of the fourteenth floor that was really the thirteenth. All the floors looked the same and, once, she'd got off on the tenth floor by mistake, and hadn't noticed until she stood in front of what ought to have been her own front door and wondered where that Cornish pixy door knocker came from.

Once inside the flat, though, she barred and bolted the door and felt safer. Mum kept everything clean and cosy, and with the lights on, and the curtains drawn, you could almost convince yourself that you were somewhere safe and homely.

Still, she put the television on for company in the empty space. Leaving it blaring loudly, she went into the kitchen to prepare her supper.

She put a pan of water on to boil for her boil-in-the-bag casserole, and then because she couldn't wait (no wonder you're so fat, my girl) made herself a large jam sandwich.

It was while she was eating her sandwich that the voice came to her from the living room.

Loud and clear, it said: 'In every city, a dozen or so other cities lie hidden.'

She put down her sandwich, and holding herself carefully, as though she were an egg, went slowly back into the living room.

In every city a dozen or so other cities lie hidden . . .

But the strangeness and shock only lasted for a few seconds. On the television an archaeological programme was in progress. A woman stood in shorts and a t-shirt amongst some sandy ruins. Debra lowered herself into a chair, and listened to the rest of what she was saying.

'We have to remember that no city is just one city. So how do we find them, those hidden cities?'

'I don't know,' Debra said out loud to the television set. 'Just how do we find them?'

'For the fact is, that we can't find one without destroying perhaps half a dozen others. Schliemann, we know, destroyed Troy several times over, before he reached the city he decided was the real one.'

'I don't want to destroy it,' Debra said. 'I just want to find it.'

The woman in shorts seemed determined to answer her. 'Sometimes the harder we look, the more elusive our lost cities seem to be. It's often only when we're not trying that we discover the key.'

'Thank you and goodnight,' said Debra, and switched over to another channel where Tom was chasing Jerry endlessly round and round, two pretend creatures in an endless pretend game.

4

The arrangement with Matthew was that they would meet by the fountain in Holland Park, at twelve o'clock the following morning.

She slept that night without the dream of the man writing, and woke up clear-headed.

'I'm meeting this boy,' she said to herself.

It was the kind of thing you expected girls to say. Doubtless Rachel Ward and Sharon Black said it all the time. Well, it was all right for them. Everything like that came easy to them. All Rachel had to do was to toss her pretty blonde hair and a dozen boys would come running. You knew she didn't have a brain in her head, and by the time she was thirty-five, she'd be washed out with half a dozen kids hanging round her. But that didn't mean that just sometimes you didn't envy her her luck.

I'm meeting this boy . . .

Of course, Matthew Best didn't really count. He was a boy, of course, but not . . . well, not the sort to get excited about.

Which was a relief. For if it had been someone else waiting there for her, Heathcliff perhaps, or the man in her dream, writing, she might have felt too nervous to go. As it was, she spent a good hour deciding what to wear, trying on clothes and taking them off again, doing her hair, up, down and several ways in between.

At any rate, it took her mind off hidden cities and all that rubbish.

She would have arrived at Holland Park too early, so she went into a supermarket near Holland Park Station, and passed ten minutes wandering round aimlessly looking at shampoos. The girl assistant was not much older than herself, blonde and of the same species as Rachel Ward. 'Was there anything *special* you wanted? No? Well, do you mind not messing up the displays then, please?' Debra shuffled out, thinking of the several brilliant remarks she could have made, if only she'd thought of them at the right time.

He was already there when she arrived at the fountain, his head down against the cold, hands thrust into the pockets of the expensive bomber jacket. He looked lost and desolate.

But his grin when he saw her was as cocky as ever. 'Hi, sexy.'

'Hi, gorgeous,' she answered, feeling that for once Rachel could have responded no better.

'Okay,' he said. 'Follow me,' and set off along the path in the direction of the side gate. Everything in the park today was frosted with cold, grey and silent, the sky milky white, the trees as still as if they had been carved from stone.

'Where are we going?'

'You'll see.'

'I don't want to see. I want to know.'

'I-am-tekking-you-avai-to-my-kingdom-in-ze-sky.'

'Is that meant to be your French accent?'

'No, it's my Dracula. Vlad to see you and all that.'

18

'I think perhaps you'd better shut up,' she said, catching him up.

'But I'm still going to take you to my kingdom in the sky.'

They turned into a wide and elegant road. A block of flats stood amid manicured lawns and trees, a glittering tower.

'This is it,' he said, and Debra noticed that his voice had fallen to a whisper and his swagger had vanished.

'Do you really live here?'

'My dad does.'

Heavy glass doors swung open before them. The floor was covered with marble, white swirled with palest grey. There was pink silk on the walls, and a huge display of pink and white flowers, lit from beneath, in a niche. A porter in a grey uniform arose from nowhere. '*Good* morning Mister Best.'

Before they could reach the lift, it opened and an elderly lady in a fur coat swept out, looking past Matthew and Debra as though they were not there. 'Ah, Mr Wilkins,' she said to the porter. 'Number Forty-three had one of their parties again last night. Do you think a tiny word might be in order?'

As the lift doors closed, Debra and Matthew looked at each other and laughed.

'She's Lady something-or-other,' he said. 'She's awful. She believes in bring back hanging and send all the blacks back to Africa. And the porter, he's even worse. I bet my dad's bribed him to keep an eye on me while he's away. I call him Uriah Heep.'

'Where is your dad?'

'In L.A., my dear. Where else? With darling Venetia.'

'Who's Venetia?'

'In theory, I suppose she's my stepmother. Actually I

just think of her as my dad's wife. I don't think she fancies the idea of a stepson, least of all a spotty adolescent one. Well, here we are.'

The lift came to a halt with the gentlest of jerks and a little gasp of machinery. The doors opened on to a wide corridor, and Debra's shoes sank into soft carpets.

He took a key from his pocket and opened a door. 'After you, madam.'

The room that spread out before her was huge and glittering. There were white carpets everywhere and the kind of furniture that you only saw in magazines, all leather and glass and metal. White silk blinds hung at the windows. The only sign of human – Matthew's – occupation, was an empty coke can on the table, and a Walkman flung on to a chair. Bronze statues stood on plinths, large canvases covered the walls. She peered closely at one over the marble mantelpiece.

'It looks like a Renoir.'

'It *is* a Renoir, my dear!'

The delicate landscape with its soft colours of rose, grass green and lamplight yellow was incongruous among all the harsh glitter. 'Does your dad like paintings?'

'He collects them. Totally different thing. Look, there's a Dufy. He had a Picasso once but he sold it because he thought the bottom was going out of the Picasso market. Now he's after a Bonnard, so I believe.'

It seemed wrong that something so beautiful could be owned by someone who did not care for it. On the grand piano were pictures of a blonde, tossing back an expensive silvery mane. 'Is that Venetia?'

'That's her. Gorgeous, isn't she?' he said in a blank voice.

'Don't you like her?'

'Oh, you don't *like* Venetia, my dear. You admire her. Anyhow, she doesn't like me, so the point's immaterial.'

Debra thought that perhaps she was asking too many personal questions, so she switched to a less tricky subject. 'How big is this flat, anyway?'

'Huge. It's the penthouse. Come on, I'll give you a guided tour. Except that you can't go into the sacred shrine itself. Venetia kindly locked the bedroom door before they went away.'

'Why?'

'Because she doesn't trust what nasty little Matthew might get up to on her silken sheets, that's why. Come on, I'll show you the kitchen.'

This was another huge room, all gleaming white cupboards and cunningly arranged breakfast bars and built-in barbecues. Matthew flung open cupboard after cupboard, and Debra saw stacks of porcelain plates, rows of crystal glasses. But there seemed to be no food cupboards. Eventually Debra found one; it contained a jar of Marmite and a packet of herbal tea.

'Want to see something really disgusting?' He opened the door of the fridge.

It was empty except for half a bottle of Perrier and a large white jar. She picked up the jar. 'Face cream?'

'Doesn't that make you want to throw up?'

'Why on earth does she keep it in the fridge?'

'To look after it. With what that jar of muck cost, you could feed an Ethiopian family for a year. I know. I saw the bill. Anyway, you asked where the meals come from. I'll show you where they come from.'

And he took her through a little door in the far side of the big kitchen, into another kitchen. This one was much smaller, and not unlike her mother's kitchen at home. There was a gas stove, a fridge, a washing machine and dryer, an ironing board. It was functional and ordinary. Beyond this second kitchen was another little room, barely a cupboard in contrast, with a narrow bed, a chair, a television. The shelf above the bed was ranged with cheap little ornaments, china cats and dolls and photographs in small gilt frames.

'This is where the meals come from. It's Maria's room. She's not here at the moment; she's gone back to Spain for Christmas. Not that Dad and Venetia have too many cosy evenings at home. But when they do, Maria scurries out of her hole, puts the food on the table, clears it up and scurries back again when nobody's looking.'

'How can she stand living like that?'

'Oh, Maria worships Venetia, who treats her like dirt, and she thinks the sun shines out of my father's bottom. Anyway, enough of this. I've put cokes and take-away pizzas in Maria's fridge. Why don't we have some lunch?'

They ate their lunch from one of the glass-topped coffee tables spread with the *Daily Mirror*. As she struggled with strings of melted cheese, Debra said, 'How long have you been living here?'

Matthew's face went very guarded. 'Not long,' he said. She noticed that he hadn't been talking in funny voices for some time now. 'My mum's away on holiday.'

They both ate in silence for some moments after this, without looking at each other. Debra was embarrassed because this was not what she had heard about his mother, and she did not want Matthew to think she was prying. He told her anyway in a few moments. 'Oh, what the hell. She's not on holiday,' he said. 'Half the kids at school seem to know. She's in this clinic.'

'I'm sorry,' Debra said stiffly.

'No, it's all right. It's quite nice to talk about it, actually. I've been so busy keeping my mouth shut. But

22

everyone thinks just because she's an alcoholic, she staggers around like a drunken bag-lady all the time. It isn't like that. Mostly, you wouldn't know. And she's tried so hard to get on top of it. She's nice, she really is. You'd like her. But this thing's killing her.' He put down half his pizza unfinished on the table. 'Anyway, there's this clinic in Warwickshire. Apparently it's really good. You spend two months there. It costs a fortune. We could never afford it. Dad's coughed up for this, which I suppose is quite decent of him, considering.'

'Considering what?'

He laughed. 'Well, considering they didn't bother getting married when I arrived on the scene. He wasn't so rich then. He was the boss and she was his secretary. I was the great mistake. Mind, I suppose it would have been an even worse mistake if they had got married. And at least he's always acknowledged me and supported me.'

'So he damn well should,' Debra said.

'Oh, that's not what Venetia thinks. I heard her once; *why didn't you put the little bastard in a home* was how she put it, I believe. Well, that's enough about my problems. Let's hear about yours for a change.' He put on a mad-Viennese-shrink voice. '*I vont to hear, my dear, all about your unhappy childhood. . . .*'

5

It was almost dark when she set off home, through a
November mist that blotted up the lights of street and
car. The air tasted metallic and sooty. If she'd been
thinking straight she would not have taken the route that
led through the twilit park, but she was not thinking
straight. Her mind was filled with Matthew and the
things they had talked about. It hadn't been a romantic
afternoon; they'd just talked, but she had never been able
to talk like that to anyone before. And, in spite of his
unkind remark in class, it seemed that he didn't just
dismiss her as Fat Debra, the Mammal. 'If I had a brain
like yours,' he'd said enviously, 'I could do anything. If
you're clever, you can be in control of your life.' She
hadn't thought of it this way. Maybe it was true.

Anyway, it would be good to have a friend. Other
people had friends. Now she might have one too.

In the park, colours swam through the murk, the black
filigree of branches, the green of the playing field, the
rosy-rust of the old house.

At first she did not notice that she was alone on the
broad tree-lined path. There was no-one else in sight.

She realised that at just the same moment when she
heard the footsteps behind her.

She stopped. The footsteps stopped.

When she started up again, so did they, slightly muffled by the fog.

Clever, eh? In control of your own life? All it takes is one loony . . .

She did not dare turn round. And should she walk faster, or slower? Should she run? He might run faster. Scream? No-one to hear.

Panic was turning her brain into porridge. All she could do was to carry on walking and walking; but when she turned a corner, the footsteps were still behind her.

And she realised that she had made the mistake of walking deeper and deeper into the park, instead of towards the street and comparative safety.

In her dazed and stupefied state, she thought she might be able to hide from the pursuer, behind a pillar or some bushes. Starting to run now, she found herself in a narrow path, winding up and away, beneath a lacework of wintry branches.

The door was just ahead, in a solid building that might be the cafeteria. It was half open, and she thought she saw a light gleaming dully through it.

She was running as fast as she could now. When she reached the door, she hurled herself through it into the thick darkness, calling 'Help me, please! There's some-one after me!'

There was no-one in the darkness to hear her.

And when she turned round, she realised that there was nobody behind her either.

Nobody, no path through the trees, no park.

It was light, that was the first thing she noticed. Not the crystal shine of moonlight, but the cool direct light of morning. There was no sun in the pale sky.

She stepped through the doorway, into the street. The doorway was flanked by carved pilasters, and the door had an iron knocker with a lion's head. She touched it. Did it really exist? It did.

Long colonnades ran in both directions, dark bronzy stone. The cobbled street was quite empty. A pile of cabbage leaves had been swept into the gutter. Doors were closed, windows shuttered. The colonnades swallowed everything in shadow, but she could make out carvings over doors and lintels. Some were broken, and others looked as though they had been taken from elsewhere and used to patch up. In the middle of a blank wall was a fragment of a face, just a nose and grinning mouth. Somewhere else she saw half a horse.

Out in the road, she looked for a sign to tell her where she was. There was nothing. She set off at random. As she came to a crossroads she saw a slender green tower in the distance over the rooftops, and recognised it as the one she had seen before. Still there was not a soul in sight, and nothing to direct her. Which was strange, for she was used to words assailing her from all sides; *Stop, Go, Coca-Cola, Coming Soon, Refreshes The Parts, Road Works Ahead, Put your Trust in Jesus, Burger Bar, Unisex, Tracey Is A Slag, Say No To Nuclear Waste* . . .

Not even a scrap of newspaper in the street. Walking through that silent curve, she might have been the only person alive in the world.

The sky shone pale and bright, with an odd greenish tinge to it. Was it morning or evening? From time to time smells wafted up to her, with a suggestion of bad drains or rotting vegetation. The air was close, and bland, much warmer than the November evening she had left behind, and dust prickled in her nostrils. But there must be dampness too, for here was a waterfall of green slime, and when she touched the wall around it, black mould came off on her hand. But she was no longer anxious. It was as though anxiety had been switched off in the November park.

Orchard Estate might have been a place in a dream. Even Matthew, to whom she had spoken so recently, now seemed like a person in another, far-away dimension. Leaving behind The Mammal, Aspen Towers, Rachel Ward, she could remake herself from scratch, a new person in a new world.

Yet surely she could not be the only person alive? People had been here recently. Here was a ladder left propped against a wall, a door half painted dark blue. An apple core, brown but showing teeth marks, was in the gutter. Someone had made those marks. A daisy in a pot on a window sill had to be watered. So where were they all?

From time to time, the green spire came into sight and then vanished. She wanted to find it, but the curve of the road seemed to be leading her away.

Finding a dark and narrow side road, she turned down, but by now she was losing her sense of direction. Another narrow road, and then another. High shuttered windows faced her blankly. Looking up at them, she nearly tripped over an old shoe, but there was no sign of its owner.

Now she turned into another colonnaded street, wide and straight. It came as a surprise when suddenly she found herself in front of a door with a lion door knocker and realised she had come full circle and arrived at the door by which she had entered.

When she pushed, it swung open a little, a heavy door, but hanging on powerful hinges. She could only see darkness beyond. There seemed nothing to do but go

27

through, and so she stepped over the threshold, and into the darkness.

6

Into darkness and raw November fog. So dark that she could hardly see where she was; but she made out trees and bushes.

When she had been here before – it seemed like an age ago – she had been running away from someone, she could remember that. What had happened?

She stood there, foolishly, in the twilight, but there was no-one there now. Her pursuer had probably given up, but you couldn't be sure of that. She began to run.

It was dark now. Surely darker than before.

At the gates, the park-keeper was just locking up. 'Didn't you hear the bell?' he grumbled. 'You kids deserve to be locked in all night, you do. Think I've nothing better to do than to run round after you.'

Still, he opened up for her, and let her into the street.

Cars swishing past in the gloom, people walking home, curtains being drawn. Just an ordinary evening.

7

The following day, Friday, she spent at home, too dazed and strange to have much energy for anything. By Saturday morning, she was more like her old self. She had almost convinced herself that she had never really gone through that door, it was all a dream. In the Orchard Estate, with the wind blowing across the forecourt and the sharp blocks of flats glittering like razors against the cold sky, it was hard to believe in any alternative reality.

She needed some shopping so she went to the supermarket at the edge of the Estate.

'Your mum not back yet?' said the girl at the checkout who knew them slightly.

'Not yet.'

'She must trust you, leaving you alone. All those wild parties you could be having!'

Debra smiled wanly. 'Well, I'm not.'

'Shame,' said the girl. 'Morning, Mrs Cole. How's your leg today?'

A weekend on your own is a long time, Debra discovered. She took the shopping home, tidied the flat, and it was still only mid-day. After a cup of tea and a sandwich, she went to the afternoon film at the Kensington Odeon, a sentimental American love story that left her unmoved.

And by three-thirty, it was over. She came back through the park. Two girls from her school were there, walking aimlessly and giggling; a park keeper swept huge piles of crackling dry plane leaves; two children roller skated.

She looked for doors set into the wall that ought not to be there. But there was only one that looked as though it might be strange, but when she rattled the handle, nothing happened except for a keeper shouting angrily, 'Hey you! That's private in there!'

Then she came up Abbotsbury Road to Holland Park Avenue. From Holland Park Avenue, she crossed by subway into Shepherd's Bush. The walls of the subway were blank and white.

On Saturday evening, she hoped Matthew would ring, but he didn't. She thought of him in the big flat and wondered what he was doing there. Suddenly full of pity for him alone in all that glitter, she looked up his father's name in the telephone directory. There it was, and the number of the penthouse. But when she rang the number, nobody answered. Matthew was not there.

Her mother rang later that evening. But she sounded too distracted by her own problems in Ireland to listen to Debra's. Things were bad; Debra's grandmother was ill, and it looked serious. She was not sure when she'd be back, but it might be a week or so. Why didn't Debra close the flat and come over?

Debra said nothing about the strike. How can I come, she said disdainfully, I have exams to work for, remember?

Sunday was a very long day indeed. She tried to get up late, but by half past eight she was wide awake. The Sunday paper occupied her half an hour, breakfast took five minutes. An Open University programme on Emily Bronte held her attention for all of thirty minutes, but when it came to the next programme about polyester resins, she thought enough was enough and switched it off. Matthew? She picked up the phone and dialled the first three numbers, but then slammed the phone down. No-one phoned anybody at half past nine on a Sunday morning. Homework took her a couple of hours, but then her head started to ache, and it was still not lunchtime. She had lunch anyway, a hamburger and frozen chips. While she was eating, the phone rang.

She rushed to answer it, swallowing down chips.

'Hallo?'

'Oh,' said a quavery voice at the other end. 'Elizabeth?'

'No. Who's that, please?'

'You aren't Elizabeth?'

'No. Who's that?'

'I wanted Elizabeth,' quavered the voice indignantly. 'You must be a wrong number.'

After that, the phone did not ring again.

In the afternoon, she went for a walk. Shepherd's Bush. Holland Park. There were no doors there that should not be there.

When Monday morning came, she was relieved to be able to set off for school. But there was a crowd at the gates. A notice read: 'We regret that as a consequence of last week's industrial action the school central heating service has suffered a breakdown. We hope to resume lessons tomorrow.'

Someone was muttering, 'It's not bloody fair, this, you know.' Another kid said, 'Great! More strikes!'

Some boys from her class came up. Mark Stacey,

Stephen Lowe. 'Hi, Mammal,' said Mark. 'We were all going down MacDonald's. Want to come?'

Debra opened her mouth. She might have been going to say yes, but then Rachel Ward strolled up. 'Oh, she won't come,' said Rachel. 'The Mammal wouldn't lower herself to go to MacDonalds with the likes of us.'

'Give the girl a break,' Stephen said mildly, but Debra felt her own smile turning to something very much like a snarl. 'I'd rather watch paint dry than talk to you, Rachel Ward,' was what she said.

She hoped they'd try and persuade her to come, but they didn't. 'Okay, please yourself,' said Rachel, and the group turned away. She heard her say, 'Hey, did anyone see Michael Jackson on last night?' and they wandered away.

Where was Matthew? She asked a third year. 'Have you seen Matthew Best?'

'Who?' said the kid.

'You his girl friend then?' said another when she asked the same question. She didn't want to make a nuisance of herself hanging around ('Hey, Matthew, there was this fat girl looking for you!'), so she stuck her hands in her anorak pockets, put her head down, and walked off rapidly in the direction of Notting Hill Gate.

8

If she went to Kensington High Street, Rachel and the rest might think she was hanging around them . . .

If she went to Holland Park, Matthew might think she was hanging around after him . . .

She had to go in the other direction.

Notting Hill Gate was where she was aiming for. But before she got there, she came to Holland Park Tube, and on an impulse, went in and asked for a ticket to Oxford Circus.

The lifts weren't working in Holland Park. It was an old station, all bottle-green tiles, and when the lifts didn't work, you had to take an ancient dark staircase, winding down and down.

The stairs smelled of darkness, of dust and the depths of the earth. Down and down. There seemed to be an awful number of stairs. No wonder they said people with weak hearts shouldn't attempt to use them. The wall curved at her elbow, peeling paintwork dingy and dark. Someone had started to write in blue spray-paint THE KIN . . . 'The King' most probably. Everyone was The King with a can of spray-paint. But the letters were broken off jaggedly.

No wonder. It was getting darker and darker. Surely the least they could do was to put a light on the stairs. Did they expect you to break your neck? It was like the Underworld here, dark and airless, the grime getting in her throat and choking her.

And how narrow the steps had become. Suppose she passed somebody; there was not room for two abreast.

Here was the door.

Was there a door at the end of the stairs? Obviously, for here it was. Strange that you couldn't hear the rumbling of the trains.

She opened the door, and walked, blinking, into daylight.

It might have been a different street, or it might have been the same. She stood in an archway, looking out.

There was the City smell, freshness mingled with the rottenness of drains and something decaying. There was bright light, slightly unnatural after the gloom, sending sharp shadows down the cobbles. But most of all, and this was what shocked her, there was noise. People rushed and shoved and called out raucously. *Her* City – her beautiful City – was full of people!

Not just a few – it was crammed and bursting with people, noisy and jostling and everywhere. And the clothes they wore, so shapeless and baggy, as though they'd run up for themselves the kind of fancy dress you made on wet Saturday afternoons out of your mother's old clothes!

The smell of hot slightly rancid fat drifted down, and she saw a girl in a long blue dress selling sausages at a roadside stall. She called out something that Debra could not understand. A big man carried a child on his shoulders. The child cried something too, in a high, excited voice.

The smell of people filled the air, mingling with the

smell of fat so that Debra began to feel slightly nauseated. Who were they all? What were they doing in *her* City?

For she had not imagined that her lovely silent City might be populated by such a noisy mob. If she had envisaged inhabitants, she had seen them as silent and graceful, robed and mysterious, gliding round corners. *This* was like a newsreel of some noisy third world city, some overcrowded melting pot.

No-one appeared to notice Debra as she stood in the shadows. She wondered how her own clothes would pass muster, having dressed this morning, as she always did, partly to minimise her size, partly to look inconspicuous. A baggy black skirt, a big grey sweater, a black nylon anorak. Apart from the anorak, it might do – just. It was hot, anyway, here; clearly she had not walked into November, so she slipped the anorak off and put it over her arm.

And she tentatively set off down the road, still keeping to the shadows. She passed the stall, where the girl briskly crammed sausages into pouches of bread.

'Kemmaluk!' cried someone. 'Kemmaluk!'

A little bandy man rolled out of the shadows opposite. He grinned at the crowd who stopped to look at him. Then he unrolled a bundle on the ground, with a flourish and a grin of bad teeth. 'Kemmasee! Kemmasee!'

Out of the bundle came three clubs, then four, then five. He showed each one to the crowd and then, when he held all five, began to juggle. Clubs showered into the air. He pretended to drop one, and as they gasped, caught it again. He changed the rhythm of the juggling, he juggled under a leg, under an arm.

Unlike the crowd, Debra was not very impressed. You

could see just as good, or better, on television any day.

'Kemmasee!' she could hear him call as she made her way through the crowds.

What were they all gathering for? For clearly some excitement was about to happen. A big man pushed past her, and then shouted something she did not understand. They all talked so fast, and in such a high-pitched monotone. A little child yelled at the top of his lungs, 'Gessakey bab, ma!'

And the mother said something back that sounded very much like 'Shurrup.'

'Wannakey bab!' insisted the child. 'Wanner!'

'Hayn no money!' said the woman. 'Ne shurrup, willyer?'

Debra realised with a shock that what they were talking was English. English of a sort, a peculiar sort that was unlike any English she had heard before, but it was English. The child wanted a kebab; the mother wouldn't buy him one because she said she had no money.

And as if to confirm this, Debra heard the girl in the blue dress calling out, 'Frashkey-babs! Ah frash!' *Fresh kebabs! All fresh!*

Well, for a start they weren't kebabs, they were sausages. And from the smell, fresh wasn't the adjective Debra would have used. And the strange high-pitched sing-song made it hard to understand.

But once she had the key, she could make out here and there a familiar word or phrase. It was like hearing things in a foreign language that you'd learned to speak from books. Nothing was quite right. And not quite wrong either.

And as if to confirm her discovery, the bandy little man started to do a conjuring trick. A coin flashed in his hand, and then disappeared. 'Now you see it!' he called above the noise of the crowd. 'Now you don't!'

But the attention of the crowd was distracted by something that was going on at the far end of the street. There was a surge and a tension among them. The little juggler rolled up his bundle and disappeared, the girl on the stall was hastily covering things up with a cloth.

'They coming now?' she heard.

'They here soon! Quick!' (It sounded like 'quack'.)

'Into line!'

'Hurry you!' This was to Debra. People were lining up now along the street.

Well, that was clear enough. She shuffled herself into place between an old lame woman leaning dottily on a crutch, and a red-faced man in an orange tunic. If anyone thought she looked out of place, no one said so, though she noticed some people looking at her curiously.

What were they waiting for? And how long would it be? It seemed to her that she stood there for ages, between the woman and the man. Once the woman turned and said something to her that Debra didn't understand. Debra smiled back and the woman seemed satisfied, for she said something else, and then turned away, peering excitedly over the crowd, her old head wobbling.

Meanwhile, the heat increased. There was no sun, just a general disseminated brightness. The sky was white, with the faintest hint of green. In the heat, the stonework glowed like polished iron, showing the intricate carvings. These were crude and heavy, with a slightly Aztec look to them. Over an archway, she noticed one she had not seen before. There was a face, round, blank, masklike. Around it flickered stylised sun-rays.

As she was looking up, suddenly something came up right in front of her. All around her people pulled away.

She saw at once the face again, the face surrounded by flames, glittering coldly.

She realised that what she was looking at now was a metal breastplate, embossed with the same image. Her eyes travelled slowly upwards. There was no face where a face should have been, only a blank helmet of some gleaming black metal, with slits for eyes. A curved flange covered nose and chin. She could not even tell whether the being was man or woman, but guessed by the height that it was a man. As well as the breastplate and helmet, he wore a black full-sleeved tunic, and black trousers tucked into shiny black boots. His hand was covered with heavy silver rings – all bearing, Debra saw, the image of the sun-surrounded face – and held a huge heavy spear, black-hafted.

He was saying something.

Debra gaped.

He repeated it. The crowd shrunk back around her.

'I don't understand.'

'Who you? What house you from?'

Me Tarzan. You Jane. In spite of her fear, Debra stifled an instinct to giggle. She thought, if only Matthew were here!

'I'm Debra,' she said carefully. 'Debra Stoner.'

The guard turned to the crowd. 'Anyone here know her?'

Their anxiety to disclaim her was almost comic. 'Never seen her,' they clamoured. 'Not seen her before. Don't know her.'

The guard stepped out into the road. 'Hey!' he called. 'Come up here, will you?'

And Debra saw that at the end of the road, which had now emptied, stood a little knot of the black-clad guards.

For once, Debra's instincts worked quicker than her brain.

Before anyone else could move, she ran.

9

Through arches and doorways she ran, scarcely aware of the crowd parting around her. Walls came up to her and fell away, windows flashed past. The cobbles were rough beneath her feet but did not deter her. She could make out nothing but the sides of the City, peeling away from her like an orange as she ran. There was a doorway; she entered, into darkness. Here dust and a thickness in the air caught her for a moment, but still she ran. She ran through the darkness, and into brightness again. The brightness almost blinded her, the sound of her feet on the ground had changed, into a hollow ringing sound. Around her, but muffled, there was a great shaking and rumbling.

And then at last she stopped running.

The Central Line train was pulling slowly away from the platform.

'Never mind, my dear,' said a pleasantly spoken woman by her side. 'There'll be another along soon.'

Breathless, Debra could hardly bring herself to smile politely. But she was grateful to the woman, after the menace of the guards and the crowds with their peculiar voices. She was grateful to find herself back amongst the familiar and predictable.

When the next Central Line train pulled in, she got on

it, still grateful, and sank down between a business man and a Japanese tourist, laden with expensive cameras. This was her city, and she knew its rules. Nevertheless, as she leaned back in her seat, looking at an advertisement for an employment agency, she felt disoriented and unreal. The feeling continued until she found herself coming up the wide subway at Oxford Circus. The crowd swarmed around her, someone thrust a free magazine into her hand, someone else bumped into her, and said, 'Sorry, love.' At the corner of Argyle Street, a man was selling frankfurters from a stall. *Fresh kebabs, all fresh*! Only he wasn't saying that. He wasn't saying anything as he handed them briskly out. A drunk was accosting passers-by, trying to get an audience for his tirade. A child called out, 'I *want* it, Mummy!'

Everything nearly the same, yet how different! What would the inhabitants of *her* city make of the buses trundling by, the glitter of the lights that were strung across the road for Christmas, at the shop windows crammed with goods?

Two cities, so near each other, and yet so far apart!

In every city, a dozen other cities might lie hidden. How do we reach them, those hidden cities?

That evening, as she sat in front of the television with a plate of spaghetti, the phone rang. She expected it to be another wrong number, but it was Matthew.

'Debra! Where were you?'

'Where was I when?'

'School this morning. I waited ages by the gates.'

'I was there. I waited too.'

'We must have missed each other. I say, chaps, you realise what this means?' he went on in World War Two Group Captain tones.

'What does it mean?'

'It means I need a new watch,' he said in his normal voice.

Debra began to feel better already. 'You are an idiot.'

'You have a good weekend?'

'Not bad,' she lied. 'How about you?'

'I went down to see Mum.'

'Oh.' So he hadn't been living it up! 'How was she?'

'Not bad. Quite good actually. She's really feeling confident she can kick it this time.'

'Great.' Debra began to relax. Things were going to be all right again.

But his next words threw her right back to square one.

'Debra, I've got something to tell you.'

'Oh?'

'The thing is, I've just had a phone call from Dad. He wants me to go over there for Christmas.'

'There?'

'You know. L.A.'

Debra kept her voice light and nonchalant. 'So what's the problem?'

'No problem really. Except . . .'

'Except?'

'Me and Dad. And the Snow Queen. Can we stand each other all that time? But Christmas in L.A! Imagine!'

'Sounds great.'

'And he knows loads of film people. All these flash Hollywood kids. I wouldn't have to get under his feet. But then . . .'

'But . . .?'

'But you know . . . we're just getting to know each other. Then I vanish.'

She could tell, though, from the tone of his voice that he wanted to go. Well, who wouldn't? Given the choice of being all by yourself, or having a wild time in the States, who wouldn't want to go? She couldn't tell him, could she, that the thought of losing just about the only anchor she had at the moment filled her with panic. 'So?' she said lightly. 'I'll still be here when you get back.'

'You don't mind me going?'

'Why should I?' That's it, Debra, keep it up. 'So when are you off?'

'Well, this is the thing, tomorrow. There's a place on tomorrow's TWA flight. I have to phone dad tonight and tell him.'

'Then you'd better get phoning right away.'

'You reckon?'

'I do.'

'Then I will. Hey, Debra?'

'What?'

'Here's looking at you, kid.'

'Here's looking at you, too.'

END THIS WICKED STRIKE, howled the papers the next morning. P.M. SAYS NO TO TEACHERS BLACKMAIL. Well, it seemed that the strikes were on again. Probably there wouldn't be normal school until January. 'I think it's disgusting,' said an angry parent on the News. 'My boy's taking exams and he's missed three weeks already, it's shocking. . . .'

Shocking or not, there it was. The school was closed again today, and would be closed the following day. Matthew was somewhere over the Atlantic Ocean. Debra wandered the streets, looking for places and people that were not there.

That night, she could not sleep. Twelve o'clock. One o'clock, two, three.

At three o'clock, she gave up the attempt. She got up,

dressed, and made herself a cup of tea. Outside, the Estate, anchored in moonlight, was silent and apparently serene. Only a few lights shone in the packed layers of dwellings. A drunk weaved his way across the forecourt and disappeared. Neon lights gave the sky a faint purplish glow. Of the murderers, rapists and crazed junkies who stalked the city after dark, there was no sign, not from the thirteenth floor, at any rate. She thought, if I were Emily Bronte now, I should go for a moonlight walk over the moors, with my dog for company, dreaming of Heathcliff, the wind in my hair.

Orchard Estate was not the Yorkshire moors, Debra was not Emily Bronte. But she decided to go for a walk anyway.

She'd never been out in the middle of the night before, and she was surprised to find that it could be done. The lift carried her down and deposited her at the front entrance, where the night sky dazzled her, and the cold wind blew in her face. She had dressed herself in a peculiar combination of things, chosen as the nearest thing to a disguise she could think of; the most shapeless of her shapeless skirts, with an old tent-like black coat of her mother's, and with a black stole thrown over her head and shoulders like a nun or an Arab woman. She wanted to be, as nearly as possible, just a black shape in the night.

Her footsteps sounded impossibly loud, and she kept turning fearfully around as she crossed the forecourt. She felt that by being out so late, she was doing something illegal, instead of merely crazy. But nobody stopped her. She crossed the Orchard, and the neighbouring Willow Farm Estate. One or two cars went by in a blaze of headlights. A couple of drunks leaning against a wall called out to her, but they were too drunk to move, and she walked briskly on.

She reached Holland Park Avenue, where the huge houses of the rich slumbered quietly behind banks of shrubs. Maybe it was only an illusion, but she began to feel quite safe, alone in the night.

Here the houses were separated from the road by high brick walls. Long gardens filled with trees ran beyond the walls in the darkness. There were doors, heavily bolted, that led into these gardens. In the dark, she had lost a precise sense of her location, so when she found the door set into a wall, she could not say exactly where it was. But she knew now that there were doors and doors. The City might be hidden, but the doors to it were everywhere. When it was time to find them, they were to be found. So she turned the handle, and walked through.

10

It was night in London, but here it was just twilight. In the silent street, shutters were being closed. As a man locked the door of his shop, a light glowed like a flower behind a window. She did not recognise the street, and there was no-one else to be seen except the man walking away from his shop. He did not see Debra.

In the distance, she could hear the sound of chanting. The sound was faint, but with that peculiar thickness and density that comes from a large number of voices in unison. Keeping to the shadows, she followed the silent, shuttered street towards its direction.

As she turned a corner, it grew louder, a monotonous chant. But she did not expect such a crowd, in so huge a space.

The street opened out into a square. This square stretched so far away that the buildings on the other side were tiny, like models. All around looped the arcades, so that you could walk it entirely beneath them. Everybody was facing the same way, turned towards a building opposite, with an elaborate carved façade, and a balcony. They were still and spellbound, every one of them, as though waiting for a miracle to happen. Even the tiny children did not fidget.

Keeping to the arches, she moved across the square. A

sudden scuffling and movement startled her; the crowd were lighting candles, though without a pause in their singing. By now, she could see the building more clearly. It was like a palace, but it was a jumble, too, as though someone had simply piled together all the ornaments they could think of; stone twisted into barley sugar spirals, gothic pinnacles, scallops and zig-zags, columns that looked Greek, others that might have been Indian. It seemed to undulate before her, all curves and spires. It was, quite frankly, a mess.

As she watched, a line of black uniformed men appeared on the balcony. The crowd gasped, and then fell silent.

The silence that now filled the square was almost as tangible as the chanting had been. They were waiting for something.

They waited five, then ten, then fifteen minutes. And then, when all were wrought to a high pitch of excitement, a figure appeared before them. He – was it he? – wore a mask of glittering silver, haloed with the sunburst pattern she had seen on the guards' breastplates. The robe was black, glittering with silver. The effect was both sinister and tawdry, like a demon in a Christmas pantomime. But when the figure raised a hand, everyone fell to the ground. Thousands of candles wavered and swerved in the gloom.

Debra knelt too, not to be conspicuous. But she peered through laced fingers.

The figure stood there, silent and motionless for about five minutes, and then it was gone.

Sinister, or silly? Perhaps both. Afterwards everything returned to noisy normality. People gathered themselves together and began to stream noisily out of the square, chattering and calling. Debra watched them go.

Then suddenly, a voice spoke just at her ear. 'They seen you. Look.'

Behind her was a little man, monkey-faced, missing a tooth, bandy-legged. It took a few seconds to recognise him as the entertainer. 'Look!' he repeated. 'Over there.'

And over there, stood a group of the black-clad guards, in the shadows like herself. They must have been there all the time, watching her.

'Follow me,' the little man said now. 'Walk behind me, quick.'

'But . . .' Debra began. He had already gone, turning into a side street, and down an alleyway.

She followed him. They went through one door at the front, and out of another at the back. They turned into dark windowless lanes, and across wide streets. Debra wondered how on earth anyone could find their way around the streets, everything was so dark and feature-less. There were narrow streets and wide, there were colonnades and arches. But they all looked like the same street to her.

She did not know how long they walked. Night was descending fast now, and it seemed that what the inhabitants of the City did when it got dark was to stay indoors.

They turned now into deserted streets among ruined and patched-up buildings. The man walked fast in spite of his bent and bandy legs. She began to be frightened in an everyday London way at what she was doing.

'Stop a minute!'

He stopped, and grinned at her. 'Nearly safe now. Nearly there.'

'Nearly where?'

'The Old Work. You see.'

'But you've got to tell me . . . I don't understand.

Where . . . who were those men. . . .'

He whistled out through his teeth. 'You talk funny,' he said. 'Don't understand.'

'*I* talk funny?' Debra said indignantly. Then she said very slowly, 'How do I know I'll be safe with you, where we're going?'

He nodded in the direction of the centre of the City. 'Think you'll be safe with *them*?' he said. 'Want to try it?'

Debra decided she believed him. 'All right. I'll follow you.'

'You want to live,' he said, 'you better.'

And he was off again, down dark and silent streets.

The girl, though, was angry. 'What you bring her here for?'

Debra recognised her as the girl from the kebab stall, in her blue dress. She was slight and small, with heavy dark hair that she wore in a braid. Her pale, pretty face, strong-browed, had something of the look of a small predatory animal, a weasel or a marten. She glowered at Debra now.

'We don't know her! No-one knows her! Why risk it?'

The juggler grinned and shuffled, embarrassed. 'They were after her, Annet. They seen her.'

'So? What's it to us? Who is she, anyway?'

'She's not the cat's mother, you know,' Debra said. Both stared at her blankly. 'I said,' she repeated, 'you don't have to talk about me as though I were an idiot.'

The juggler had brought her to a dark building in a street that was all ruins. They had climbed winding wooden stairs, and entered a circular room, dark and dingy, with dusty light drizzling through a little half-shuttered window. And it was cold, too; a smell of dead ashes came from the grate.

'You talk funny,' said the girl. 'I can't understand you.'

There seemed little point in arguing this. 'I'll try and speak slowly.'

'So who are you?'

'My name's Debra. Debra Stoner.'

They looked at each other and shrugged. 'What house you from?'

'I come from the Orchard Estate, White City.'

'White City! What's White City?'

'I can't explain. I'm sorry.'

'Everyone knows their house, where they're from. How come not you?'

'I don't know.'

'Did you escape?'

'Escape?'

'From the Farms. You escape?'

'No,' said Debra. 'I told you, I can't explain it.'

'I can't handle this,' the girl said. 'Cal must see her.'

The suggestion seemed to relax the little man. 'He'll know,' he said. 'He'll know what to do.'

'You must stay here. You'll come to no harm. Unless . . .'

'Unless what?'

The girl did not finish her sentence. 'Leave it for Cal,' she said. 'He'll know.'

Debra opened her mouth to argue, but it was pointless. She thought, the thing to do is to go along with them until there's a chance to find that street again and the door back.

But when it seemed that what they intended to do was to leave her there, locked in the dark little room with only a candle, she wondered if that was such a good idea after all.

She could hear them talking outside the door. There were footsteps and then silence.

'Did you do this?'

'What?'

'I said, did you do this?'

They had, after all, not left her alone for very long. Half an hour, perhaps. In her nocturnal flight, Debra had left her watch behind. And then the girl had returned, with a jug of something and a bowl of something else. Whatever was in the bowl was not very tempting.

At first Debra had looked for a way out. But she was not Houdini, the door was locked, and judging from the view over the rooftops, the room was high up. Then she searched the room for clues about the City and its people. She expected to find scraps of newspaper, letters, an old book, anything, but there was nothing. Apart from a spindly table and chair, the room was empty. In the end, she waited by the window, the candle flickering on a little table. The window was coated with dirt, and she amused herself by idly writing her name in the grime.

DEBRA STONER DEBRA.

And then, because there was no way he would possibly know she had written it.

MATTHEW. . . .

It was at this point that the girl returned. She put the tray down on the table. The writing on the window transfixed her, thrown into relief by candlelight against the dark night. 'Did you do that?'

'I don't see the crowds of other people.'

Jokes didn't seem to go down too well in the City. The girl peered closely at the writing on the window.

'What's this?'

'What does it look like?'

The girl turned a pained and slightly puzzled look in Debra's direction. It occurred to Debra that perhaps she could not read. She said, more gently, 'It's only my name, Debra.'

The girl reached out a tentative finger, touched the writing and then withdrew as though she feared it would bite.

'This is writing?'

'Yes.'

'How did you learn?'

'I can't remember.'

'Palmer, come here,' called the girl. 'Look at this.'

The two of them stared at her untidy scrawlings as though they were some exquisite masterpiece.

'Writing?' whispered Palmer.

'Read it,' commanded the girl.

Debra pointed to her name. 'That's Debra. And that's Stoner.'

'And that?'

But Debra had no intention of compounding her idiocy by reading Matthew's name out loud. 'That's nothing,' she said firmly, and started to rub it out. MATT went.

'Don't do that!'

'Why not?' And she obliterated HEW. 'Shall I write your name?' she said, to distract them from her desecration.

The girl did not answer.

'It's Annet, your name?'

A nod.

Debra wrote it, on the glass, just as it sounded. ANNET.

'And yours?'

The little man giggled like an excited child. 'I'm Palmer. My name's Palmer.'

Debra was running out of dirty glass. But she wrote, PALMER.

'Or it could be this. I don't know.'

PARMA.

This was a mistake. The girl said angrily, 'You're lying!'

'No, I'm not!'

'You said you could write.'

'So I can.'

'Palmer has only one name. Now you try to say he has two!'

'No, I'm not. I don't. Look . . .' Debra opened her mouth, and then closed it again, deciding that she was not about to embark on the problem of English orthography. Come to think of it, there were at least two other ways of spelling it. Anyway, she rubbed out the second. 'That spells Palmer, now.' For it seemed to be not at all a good idea to make the girl angry.

But they were not angry now. Instead, they both stared at the writing and at each other, as if they could not decide what to do.

Finally Annet said, 'We'll wait for Cal. He'll know.'

11

She had a long wait. The evening wore on and became night. From her little window, Debra could see the merest sprinkling of lights in the distance.

Palmer kept watch outside the door. He smiled whenever she asked questions. This seemed to be what he had been instructed to do, but it was intensely irritating.

'How long will I have to wait?'

Smile.

'Who's Cal, anyway?'

Smile.

'What's going on in this place? Why is everyone so frightened of the soldiers?'

Smile.

Debra gave up.

Then she tried blandishment. 'If you brought me some paper and a pencil, I could write something nicely.'

'No paper.'

'Then how do you . . .' Write, she was going to say. 'You must have something like paper. Cardboard, wood. And anything will do for writing. Look, a piece of charcoal from the fire.'

This did seem to rouse Palmer's interest. But the walls were panelled with dark, shiny wood, and the only surface she could find was the floor of sanded boards.

'I can write whatever you like.' In fact, what she wrote was, THIS IS BORING.

Still, it seemed to loosen Palmer's tongue, just a bit. 'You have to wait. Don't worry. You're safe with us. This is the Old Work, no-one comes here.'

'Who are you all?'

'People who hate the Guardians. They killed my family. I'm the only one left.'

'Who are the Guardians?'

He laughed incredulously. 'You saw.'

'The soldiers?'

'Guardians.'

'Who do they guard?'

'You know that.'

'I don't.'

'You must do. You saw.'

'The man in the mask?'

He appeared to find this question too foolish to be bothered with. She had to repeat it. 'The man in the mask. Who is he?'

'Really, you're not from here?'

'Really.'

'That was the Lord. The God-King.'

At last, it seemed that an explanation might be forthcoming. But then at that same moment, there was a movement on the stairs outside her room. Palmer went to see. Debra heard voices, and someone entered.

Was this the famous Cal?

It was not. Apparently the red-haired man and the dumpy girl had been brought there simply to witness the miracle of writing. Debra's fame had spread. She had to write out their names too, on the floorboards, when they had finished marvelling. MAXON, and LIN.

Maxon and Lin were more relaxed than Annet. 'Not

from the City?' exclaimed Lin. 'Are there people, not from the City?'

'Well, she isn't a horse,' said Maxon.

At last, a joke, though admittedly not a very good one. But they all laughed, even Annet.

She waited for one of them to tell her she talked funny. It was Lin who did.

'You talk funny.'

'I don't. You talk funny,' she replied.

They took it as a joke, and roared hilariously. But she was growing used to their way of talking, and it no longer struck her as strange. Give her a few more hours here, and she might be talking like that too. In fact, she probably did already.

Joking, though, as severe Annet reminded them, was not what it was about. What it *was* about, no-one had told Debra yet. 'Am I a prisoner?' she said.

'It's for your own good,' snapped Annet.

'What chance do you think you'd have, out there?' Palmer said, more reasonably. 'They know you're here now. They'll want to find you.'

'Besides,' said dumpy Lin, 'don't you *want* to meet Cal?'

What the time might be by London standards, she had no idea. Here it was getting late. Maxon and Lin had to get 'back', wherever that was. Annet and Palmer could stay 'here'. So too would Debra. When the other two had gone, Palmer brought in a folding canvas bed and blankets. Supper, it seemed, had been and gone. Luckily, she was not hungry. She had some embarrassing moments, though, trying to find the right term for 'lavatory', but the City people were less mealy-mouthed than Londoners, and Debra eventually found what she was looking for, referred to with medieval bluntness as the 'pisshouse'. It was in a dark and smelly fragment of courtyard downstairs – it was not only the word that was medieval, Debra discovered to her distaste.

But she was very tired. The sleepless night before, and all the strangeness since, had its result in a wave of exhaustion. She lay down on the bed, and before she had a chance to discover that the bed was narrow and uncomfortable and the blankets far from clean, she fell profoundly asleep.

She awoke to dusty sunlight streaming through the window, and a wooden bowl of something that looked like glue. 'Porridge,' said Palmer. 'Come on, it's good. Cal is here now. He wants to see you.'

It tasted like glue, too. Debra ate a few mouthfuls for politeness' sake. Then she attempted to clean and tidy herself up. She was in no hurry to meet the famous Cal; her plan, in so far as she had one, was to get someone to take her back to the part of the City which she knew, and look for a door to take her back.

But Annet would brook no dawdling. 'Cal is here!' she repeated. 'Hurry!'

From the window, she could see for the first time the jumbled roofscape of the City. The buildings nearby were nearly all in ruins, but in the distance she could make out gables and pinnacles. She thought she could see in the distance the narrow green spire she had observed on her first visit. 'What's that tower?' she said to Palmer. But in reply Palmer merely giggled, as though he thought she could not be so ignorant, and was asking to test him.

Annet's bullyings finally paid off. 'Come on,' she said.

'Where are we going?'

'Not far. You'll see.'

They went down the stairs, along a dark corridor and

up some more. A narrow passage, a courtyard, more stairs. To her surprise, these were wide and elegant. The ceiling had once been painted, and there were fragments of rose, almond green and gilt to be seen amid the flaking plaster. Here was a wide passage that must once have been hung with green silk, though now no more than a few fragments remained, faded to grey. Annet stopped before a pair of double doors. As she pushed them open, shards of gilt shivered to the floor.

Debra saw a great floor, and high windows through which the sunlight slanted. Many of the glass panes had been broken, and repaired with wood, with parchment, with tin, so the room was not as light as it was intended to be. Dark silvery mirrors lined one wall, making mysterious perspectives. The ceiling was encrusted with delicate plasterwork, much of which had crumbled away.

At the end of the room, a man stood looking out of the window. It seemed he had just arrived from a journey, for he wore a dark cloak and high boots. As Debra crossed the expanse of floor, her footsteps ringing, he turned slowly to look at her.

'Well,' he said with a smile, as she approached, 'so this is our magic girl.'

She had expected someone tall, from the awed way in which they'd talked about him, but he was not much taller than she was. He was older, too, than most of the people she had met, perhaps in his thirties. His high forehead, from which the dark hair was receding, and his arched nose, gave him something of a birdlike air. The brilliance of his eyes as he smiled unnerved her.

Clumsily she held out her hand. 'I'm Debra,' she said.

He did not take her hand. Perhaps here they did not shake hands.

'Debra who writes,' he said. He looked her up and down.

'She does,' Annet said. 'Or says she does.'

'I've seen it,' he said. 'I came into your room while you were asleep. Does that make you angry?'

'No.' But it did. Uncomfortable.

'We've only her word for it, that that's what writing looks like.' Annet of course. Debra turned to glower at her, and defend herself. But Cal did it for her.

'I can see no reason not to take her word. She doesn't look like a liar.'

'I'm not,' Debra said.

'Where did you learn to write, Debra?'

She opened her mouth, and shut it again. Alma Road Mixed Infants was the answer, but how would that go down here?'

'She isn't going to tell us!' Annet snapped. 'I told you, they sent her here. She must be a spy. She must.'

'I'm not a spy!' Debra said. Eyes narrowed and full of rage, Annet looked more like a little weasel than ever.

Cal put a hand on her shoulder. 'Calm yourself. If she's a spy, we'll find her out. Now, I'm cold and hungry, dear girl. I've been on the road all night. See what you can find for breakfast, will you?'

Obediently, Annet went. Debra and Cal were alone in the high, empty room. 'She doesn't like me,' Debra said.

'She will,' said Cal. He sounded so certain, you could not disbelieve it. 'Look.'

And from under his cloak, he pulled out a fragment of wood. It seemed to have been pulled away from a door or panel, for there were swirls of carving on it. But on the other side where the wood was pale and smooth, somebody had marked it crudely with charcoal. It took her several seconds to realise that they were letters. He placed the pieces of wood reverently in her hand, and she read what he had written.

T HISIS BORI N. . . .

'While you slept,' he said, 'I copied this. Have I done it well?'

Debra blushed. 'Yes. It's fine.'

'But I can't read it.'

'No.'

'Will you tell me what it says?'

Debra would have given anything not to have to.

'It's nothing. It's silly.'

'It isn't silly to me, Debra.'

'It is. I was just playing about. Look, let me write you something properly.'

'Is this secret?'

'No. Just silly.' She told him anyway. She had to explain 'boring'. It seemed to be a concept unknown in the City. Luckily, he laughed.

'Why can't you read and write?' she said, trying to cover her embarrassment.

'The question should be, how is it you can?' he said thoughtfully. 'People could once, we know that. And then did no more. All the books went. Were they destroyed? I don't know. Now reading is forbidden. Only a few still know how to do it. And they keep the secret to themselves.'

'Why?'

'What you read tells you how things are, how things were, isn't that so?'

'I suppose so, yes.'

'Destroy the books, and you destroy the past. It's as simple as that. Now they tell us only what they want.'

'Who are *they*?'

He looked hard at her, as though he was searching her

face for something. 'Annet says, Debra, that you were found here. That you can't say where you came from.'

'No. At least I can, but it doesn't make sense.'

'Tell me.'

'I came through a door from somewhere else, and ended up here.'

At that moment, as if on cue, the double doors opened, and Annet came through bearing a tray. 'There's broth here, and bread. She's had hers.'

'You're too kind,' Debra said. Annet looked at her. Did they recognise sarcasm?

'We don't have much to go round. What we give you, we take from our own mouths.'

Cal laid a hand on her arm. 'Debra will repay us.'

'How?' Annet said sulkily.

'She will teach me to write,' he said.

12

There were many things that Debra was never to find out, neither then nor later. She never did get to know why the building in the empty part of the City was so grand. Had it been a royal palace, a millionaire's mansion? No-one knew, nor were they interested. No-one else comes here, they said, so it suits us. Nor did she discover just how many people used it, coming through a network of alleys and underground passages. Mostly those who came had good reason for secrecy. Debra learned that if you offended the Guardians – and there were many ways to offend – you might disappear. Some people were tortured and killed in the honeycomb of dungeons beneath the fantastic palace in the square, others were spirited away to places outside the City that those inside it had only heard about. They were called the 'Farms'. Some were real farms, some were factories. But all that anyone knew of them was that if you went there, you might as well be dead.

And over it all ruled the God-King, the Lord. He had no name; he was just the God-King. When Debra asked about him, she received embarrassed laughter and strange looks. Even though they hated him, he had been a central part of existence for so long that the words to describe him were not there.

Cal, as usual, provided the most helpful answer when she asked the question at lunch that first day. Lunch was dry black bread and sour cheese, eaten on a rough table downstairs. Cal, Annet, Palmer, and another man called Smiv were there.

'Annet,' Cal said, 'tell Debra the Creed.'

Annet scowled. 'Must I?'

'You must.'

'But I hate saying it so much.'

'It can't hurt you now. Go on.'

You did not argue with Cal. Annet pulled a face, swallowed a mouthful of bread and began, in a blank automatic voice as though it was something long ago learned by rote:

The Lord created the City and the people of the City when the world was still new. But then people grew wicked and forgetful of his love. There was sin and evil at large in the City. Then the Lord was mindful to destroy the work he had created and all men in it. But they saw their transgression and begged for his forgiveness. So the Lord said, "I shall come and live among you as one of your own, and I shall guide you and care for you as a father cares for his children, so that there will no longer be fear and evil in my City." And he came down, and since that day, the people of the City have been blessed by his presence, and guided by his rule. . . .'

Annet stopped. 'Cal, you promised us that no-one would ever have to say that again.'

'Do you have to learn it?' Debra said.

Annet threw her a look of scorn. She rolled back her sleeve. On her forearm was a silvery scar about three inches long. 'See that? I was six when our class had to learn it. I knew it all right, my mother made sure of that, but half-way through saying it, I got frightened and forgot the words. That was my punishment; I was branded with a hot poker.'

'So you see, Debra,' Cal said, 'how they make us learn what they want. But it's easier to kill people than to kill their stories. And though they've tried their hardest to wipe out the stories, they still get told.'

'What are the stories?'

'We hear of a time before God-Kings and Guardians, when people had freedom. Books with the history of the world. The true history, not the version they give us. And then there was a time when all of this was somehow destroyed, we aren't sure how, and how gradually the Guardians and the God-King took over what remained, and tried to wipe out all memories of another way of life. We hear that the God-King is no immortal spirit, but simply a man like any other, that he dies like everyone else, and another man takes his place.'

'Doesn't any one ever see the God-King?'

'Only the Lord Guardians, the ten men of the Council of Guardians. They control everything in the City. For the rest of us, we see him four times a year, as you saw him, masked and at a distance.'

'We don't know what he's like, beneath that mask,' said Smiv, a big, swarthy young man. 'He could be anyone! He could be me!' And he guffawed loudly at the thought.

'They want us afraid,' said Cal. 'They keep us afraid. Then they can do what they want to us.'

'Not for ever they won't,' Palmer said. 'We'll get the better of them one day! You'll see.'

'One day,' Cal said. 'But we aren't strong enough yet. We must build up our strength and our numbers, and then . . . Debra, will you help us? We need things that you can teach us.'

For a moment, Debra thought, I know where you live, I know your names and your faces. If I said no, would you really let me go?

But such a thing seemed disloyal. After all, they looked at her with such warm smiles, especially Cal. When someone looked straight at you like that, it was difficult to refuse. Besides, she thought, I'd like to help. The Guardians sound horrible, and all that stuff about the God-King has to be rubbish. Why shouldn't they know the truth?

'I'd love to help,' she said.

In the course of that day, the word spread that Debra was there, and many of Cal's people came to see her. She met Peto, Jan, Hood, Liss, Mara, Dick, Shon, Mal, Christa. Everyone was intensely curious about her; they prodded and poked her, as though they were not sure that she was real, and examined her clothes. The St Michael label in her sweater fascinated them. 50% WOOL, 50% POLYESTER? Explain. MACHINE WASHABLE? How can a machine wash? Explain, too. (Debra's sweater actually carried instructions in French and English, she discovered now, though she'd never noticed this before; something to do with the Common Market, she supposed – but the City dwellers seemed to have no concept that other languages could exist. How can people in different places speak differently? Why don't they all speak the same? Don't they want to speak the same? Only Cal listened, alert, bright-eyed, as though he was taking in everything she said.) A 49 bus ticket caused interest too; what was a bus? What pulled it? What was a 'Fare Stage'? She realised that this was the first writing that any of them had seen. Her crumpled bus ticket was passed round like a sacred relic.

Then she had to write out all their names. There was no paper, and they insisted on using the lovely white-painted wooden panelling. It seemed a pity, but she had to comply.

The questions did not stop. She came from London, where was London, how did she get here? Did they have Guardians in London? Did they know about the God-King? Did she have a machine to wash? Did she have a bus? How did she know about the City? How did she get here?

Which of course was back to square one. 'I don't know how I got here. I just did. I don't understand it either.'

Cal, seemingly the font of all knowledge, was looked to for an explanation. But he did not have one either. All he said was, we know how to travel through distance; perhaps there are people who can travel through other dimensions as well.

Then he said something that startled her, sounding as it did, rather like what the woman on television had said: 'Perhaps there are many Cities. Perhaps we can visit all of them, if we can only find the entrances.'

It was no explanation, but it was as good a one as Debra was to find.

Later, the conversation progressed to other matters. Cal had heard, in those whispered stories, of machines which could kill. 'If we had one of those, we could get rid of them all, Guardians and God-King.' But when Debra looked horrified, he laughed. 'This isn't the time to talk of destruction. We'll overcome the God-King in time. What I'd like to know about is books. Tell us about them. Can you all own books? What do they look like?'

The day wore on and gradually it grew dark. Annet

brought candles. Then somebody said: 'This is a special day for us, with Debra here. Let's have a celebration! Let's have a party!'

This was felt to be a good idea, and even Annet, whatever she may have thought, did not dissent. The women went off to prepare food, the men brought barrels of beer. The Guardians, it seemed, did not mind people getting drunk, as long as they stayed in their own houses. Maybe it was seen as a way of keeping people quiet. More came, and names and faces began to blur. But everyone seized Debra by the hand. 'Now that you're here,' they said, 'it'll be wonderful! It's a lucky sign that you're here!'

Later, trestle tables were put up in the ballroom. Food was put out, sausages, bean soup, noodles and bread, and somebody began to play a guitar. Palmer danced and did tricks that had everyone in stitches. Lin, who had a lovely voice, sang a sad song about a vanished lover, and then a happy one about summer. Everyone began to dance, and Debra joined in. She felt, as she danced, completely happy. 'These people are my friends,' she thought. 'They want me, they're glad to see me.'

And as she danced, and drank beer, and sang, and laughed, she thought, 'Nobody at home gives a damn about me. No-one there really cares if I live or die. Even Mum; she'd rather have her Irish family any day. And Matthew – he couldn't wait to get away. Why should I care about any of them? Why should I ever go back?'

13

'It must be lucky for us, having you here,' said Lin the following day. She was peeling turnips, and throwing them into a huge soup pan.

'Why?'

'Because you can read. And besides, you found us, didn't you? That was lucky. You might have found all sorts of other people, but you didn't.'

'I hope so,' Debra said. They all assumed, Cal's people, that she would want to stay. Not one had asked whether she wanted to go back, or whether anyone at home would be missing her. Not that Debra minded. Perhaps they were taking her for granted a little; but sometimes it was nice to be taken for granted.

'Things will change now, you'll see. You'll teach Cal to read, and then he'll find out what happened to the books; he'll tell people what the Guardians are really like, and once people know how they've been tricked, they'll rise up in revolt.'

It all sounded so simple. Could reading really bring so much?

Lin finished the last of the turnips and started on potatoes. Debra was suddenly seized with remorse. 'Let me help.'

But Lin firmly shook her head. 'No.'

'Why not?'

'Cal's orders.'

'What are his orders?'

'You aren't to do any hard work. You're special. We're to look after you.'

Debra wondered what Annet felt about this. 'But I don't mind helping. I really don't.'

But Lin was not to be budged. 'We're to look after you. That's what Cal says.'

There was no paper to be had in the City. Where ordinary people had to keep records, they used wooden tallies or tied knots in string. Debra thought about all the things she could use to write on; someone remembered a piece of panelling painted dull grey that was stored downstairs. And there was chalk, used by carpenters and dress-makers. Everything else she would have to extemporize. In the old days, she thought, people managed without pads of paper and Shakespeare never had a biro. The trouble with being a twentieth-century being was that you knew everything and nothing. No good talking about televisions, or vacuum cleaners or calculators, if you could not explain how they worked. As for paper, Debra knew it was something to do with compressed wood fibres, but little more than that. There was papyrus, too, but papyrus only grew along the Nile, didn't it? Perhaps at a pinch, she might be able to make a quill pen, but what on earth did you do about ink? Still, she explained the concept of paper and ink to Peto, who was the most ingenious among them, and he went off somewhere quietly to set about inventing them.

Meanwhile, it seemed that everyone was to treat her as a queen. 'Debra, are you warm? Are you comfortable?' It was nice.

Even Annet now spoke to her with a curious formal politeness. Debra suspected she was acting under orders, but it was an improvement on her previous behaviour.

They explained to her that now the Guardians had seen her, it would be dangerous for her to walk in the City, except at night, when she could hide from the patrols. This was sad, to be deprived of her City, almost as soon as she had discovered it. But when they told her how the Guardians treated people who couldn't give an account of themselves, she thought it was for the best. So she was to stay in the palace in the Old Work, which they called the Hidden House.

Living in the Hidden House had its problems, too. No fires could be lit during the day because of the smoke, and candles were only allowed when the shutters were tightly closed. Debra could wander at will among the warren of corridors and stairways and rooms, but she must not go outside, unless someone was with her. Other people came and went; Palmer and Annet, for example, still worked in the City. Lin and some of the others were refugees who must stay in hiding, but they were not always in the Hidden House. At the moment, Lin told her, the number of Cal's people was small, and the Guardians had no idea that the organisation existed. But soon they must increase, and find somewhere outside the City where they could settle and build up their strength. Cal meanwhile worked ceaselessly; no-one knew everything that he did, or where he went.

Today, though, he was here, in the Hidden House.

And when he sent for Debra, she found him, in the ballroom, studying Debra's crude charcoal scratchings. As she entered, he smiled up at her.

'I tried to make a writing myself, once,' he said. 'A picture for every word. You'd have laughed, I expect. All those pictures! Easy enough when you want to write "man" or "flower". But how do you do "empty" or "along" or "power"? After a while I gave up.'

'I think writing was like that once. And some still is.'

'It's clever, the way it works,' he said. '*CAL*. A *c*, an *a*, and an *l*. Simple, once you think of it. So, to make *cat*, you write *c*, *a*, and something else.'

He was learning fast, Debra thought. She prayed that she'd be clever enough to teach him properly. 'I'd better show you all the letters today,' she said.

The first day went better than she'd expected. By the end of the morning, he knew the names of most of the letters and the sounds they made; and he had written a few simple words; *man, dog, sun.* Moreover, Debra had a brainwave. It was thinking about her Scrabble set that gave her the clue, and no sooner had she mentioned her idea at lunch, than Shon, who was the carpenter, had hurried off to his workshop to make her the little wooden tiles she suggested. By the evening, there was a huge box of them, all beautifully shaped and polished, and she set about painting letters on them. Some tiles were left over, and she did not think it strange that several people sidled up furtively to her, and asked her to write their names on them. She did *PALMER, MAXON, JAN, PETO.* It did not occur to her at first that they did not ask when Cal was in the room, but the following morning, she mentioned it indirectly. 'When are the others going to learn to read?'

The question did not discompose him. 'All in good time, Debra. Reading is powerful magic; it would be wrong to give it to them until the time is right.'

'When will that be?'

'Don't let that worry you. I'll decide that.'

But for some reason, things did not go so well today, in spite of her Scrabble tiles. This time, Cal decided which words he wanted to learn, and they were not the right ones to choose for the second day of learning to read. He wanted *City*, and was then irritated with her, because it began with the same letter as *Cal*. Why wasn't it *Sity*? And *write*: why should it begin with a *w*? And why *Old Work* and not *Old Werk*? Debra simply didn't know, and she had a hard time convincing him that the irregularity lay not in her teaching, but in the language itself. After a while, though, Cal's irritation lessened, and soon, he was making fun of her for her inevitable reply; 'I don't know why. It just *is*.'

The weather that day was grey and rainy – she could see from the window the ruined streets through gusts of grey driving mists. In the distance she could just see the thin green shaft of the tower she had noticed on her first day in the City. She had asked Palmer about it once. It was called the Poison Tower, he said, though he did not know why.

Meanwhile rain fell endlessly, burnishing the cobbles to pewter and bronze, and running in dirty streams in the gullies. Rainwear was non-existent, though Cal had a cloak of oiled silk; everyone else wore ordinary clothes and grumbled as they came in soaked. There was a large gathering that afternoon; Cal planned to rescue from jail a schoolteacher who had just received sentence of death for heresy. This in itself would not be too hard; through complacency and habit, security in the City had become slack of late; but the problem was not to bring suspicion on his people. Ways and means were discussed, but someone had fault to find with every plan. The atmosphere that evening was gloomy.

It became worse at supper. This time the problem was

different; Maxon came in roaring drunk, and flung himself around the room shouting and swearing. When eventually he was made to sit down, he burst into noisy sobs. Lin meanwhile went around serving the meal of bean stew and black bread, tight lipped.

Later, Debra carried dirty plates into the kitchen where Annet and Mara were washing up. This time they did not tell her she was too magic to work, and she dried up as they washed. Mara was a tall, gangling girl with sandy fair hair and freckles. During the day, she took turns with Annet on the sausage stall. 'What was the matter with Maxon tonight?' Debra asked, while Annet was busy at the other side of the room, putting away the big jars of dried beans.

'Him? Oh, he's just angry with Shon.'

'Why Shon?'

Mara sighed, and attacked a saucepan vigorously with a handful of sand to clean it. 'Maxon and Lin have been lovers for ages now, and I suppose he thought he'd got her for good.'

'But he hadn't?'

'Well, Shon and Lin have been getting pretty close recently. It's been obvious to the rest of us for weeks now. But Maxon, he's a bit slow. It's only just dawned on him.'

'So he's jealous?'

'I think he'd kill Shon if he got the chance.'

'But surely it's up to Lin, isn't it?'

'What do you mean?'

'People change their minds. If she's grown tired of Maxon, then better to call it off now, I'd have thought.'

In reply, Mara simply giggled. Debra had noticed that particular giggle before in the City; it was not a sign of amusement so much as embarrassment. They thought she was talking nonsense, but did not want to be rude

74

enough to say so. Her attempts to describe electric power had brought the same reaction the other day.

But now Annet stood behind them, her little face ferocious. When she spoke to Debra all the awkward politeness had gone. 'What do you know about anything here?' she hissed. 'You don't understand how we do things. You think you're so wonderful, talking about writing, and machines that wash, but you don't understand us; and you never will!'

14

Two busy days for Debra were followed by two empty ones. Cal, Annet and most of the people were not to be seen; they were busy with the rescue plan for the schoolmaster. Debra was left alone with Maxon who was too depressed and gloomy to talk, so there was nothing to do but wander through the passages of the Hidden House or stare at the jumbled skyline with the green tower until she knew it by heart.

The drama of Lin, Maxon and Shon continued. Lin wandered miserably around, bursting into tears when anyone spoke to her. For a few days, the little drama was overshadowed by a bigger one: the schoolmaster was found dead in his cell before he could be rescued, and Cal was angry and taciturn. There were no more reading lessons for a while.

One evening, as the girls were preparing the table for supper, Debra heard a disturbance in one of the outer rooms. Annet and Mara exchanged glances but did not say anything. A few moments later, Shon came in, grey-faced, and having difficulty with his breathing. One of the others tried to comfort him, and after a while, he staggered out again. Then Maxon came in. Red-faced and bull-like, he hunched himself furiously around the room, at last sitting down at a corner bench, from where he stared morosely at the ground.

That was when Lin reappeared. She flung herself into the room, hair dishevelled, and ran at Maxon. 'How could you! How could you!' she shouted, pummelling him with her fists and tearing his hair. He was twice her size, but she was so angry that at first he could not defend himself. Mara and Annet had to pull her away. Maxon staggered to his feet, and glared at her, rubbing his head. 'I'm going,' he said. 'I don't give a damn, anyway.'

'You don't care,' screamed Lin. 'You don't care for me at all! Don't you know what you've done? How could you, Maxon, how could you?'

'I'm off,' he said. 'You two can go to blazes for all I care.'

And he left the room, while Lin collapsed into bitter sobs. Meanwhile everyone had gathered in the room, except Cal and Shon. Nobody said very much. 'What's happened?' Debra asked, but all she got were shifty looks and silence.

Mara led the weeping Lin away. As she left the room, she shouted at Debra, 'It's all your fault! You made this happen!'

'What did I make happen?' Debra said. 'I don't understand.'

But still nobody would answer. In the end it was Annet.

'Do you really not know what she means?'

'No.'

'Then you're more of a fool than I thought. She thinks Shon is going to die. Shon thinks so, too, so he probably will.'

'So why is it my fault?'

Somebody behind her giggled, the embarrassed City giggle. Annet grabbed Debra by the arm and pulled her away.

'She thinks Maxon has put a spell on Shon,' she hissed at Debra.

'But that's nothing to do with me.'

'Oh no? Didn't you write Shon's name for Maxon the other day?'

'Yes, but . . .'

'Well, why do you think he wanted it?'

'I haven't the foggiest idea.'

'For a hex, you fool. Bad magic.'

'But it was just his name written on a piece of wood!'

Annet shrugged. 'Maxon wanted that name because it was his enemy's name.'

'Are you telling me that you think names can work magic?'

'Why do you think everyone wanted you to write their names?'

'A name's just a name. Nothing else.'

'That's not what they think.'

'But you don't believe that, surely.'

Annet studied her through narrowed dark blue eyes. 'I believe what Cal tells me. He says it's superstition.'

'Then tell them that! Writing isn't like that at all! It's just a way of putting down what people say, nothing more.'

'You may know that. I may know it. Cal does.'

'So tell the others!'

'Didn't I tell you you don't understand people here? They think you can make witchcraft with words. They think that's why they aren't allowed to read. They think that's why Cal wants to learn himself. Everyone trusts Cal; they know Cal wouldn't use magic against them. But then you come along and write things for anyone who asks. And you're surprised when it goes wrong.'

'But you can't hold me responsible because people think stupid things.'

78

'Yes, you walk in and out of our lives, just as you choose, don't you, playing the goddess with all your superior wisdom. Well, I don't know where you come from, or how you got here. But wherever it is, I don't think you're anybody important there. And you don't belong here, either.'

'You're just jealous. Just because Cal wants to spend time with me, you're jealous! You can't bear to see him giving his attention to anyone else!'

And it seemed to her afterwards that the silent fury with which Annet stared at her, as she said this, and the way in which she turned on her heel and stormed out of the room only proved the point of her words.

The following day, Cal seemed far less worried about the witchcraft business than Annet had done.

'You can't dismantle ideas all at once,' he said. 'They become fixed. It'll take time to uproot them, but it'll happen.'

'So how is it that you understand, if they don't?'

He shrugged, and smiled his slow smile, spreading out his hands. His skin was pale and freckled. The loose black shirt he wore today made him look paler than ever. 'Perhaps because I've spent so much time trying to disentangle truth from lies,' he said. 'It's been my life's work.'

'How do you find things out, if they destroy books, and tell you what to believe?'

'You can't kill truth altogether, though you can try. Truth lives on, though in all sorts of strange disguises. At school, they teach us the stories they want us to learn, about the God-King, and his battles with his enemies, about the goodness of the Guardians and the gratitude of the people, and all that stuff. But if you listen hard, you can hear other things; children, for example, have songs and stories that they only tell when they think no-one's listening, and those stories still tell bits of the truth that the Guardians try to conceal. And I think that somewhere, too, the books still exist. I don't think they've all been destroyed.'

'So where are they?'

'Well, I told you about those secret children's rhymes. One of them goes:

> *The prison yard*
> *Is the place of spooks;*
> *The Poison Tower*
> *Is the place of books. . . .'*

'The Poison Tower! That's the green tower that you can see all over the City!'

'Exactly.'

'And you think that's where they keep the books?'

'I'm certain of it.'

'Why do they call it the Poison Tower?'

'I expect it's because people always associate the colour green with poison.'

'Is it kept locked?'

'And guarded. But I've got a plan . . . Never mind, Debra. We're wasting time. Now, I think we were up to the letter *G*, weren't we? I know, let's start with *Guardian*.' He reached for a handful of letter tiles and began to arrange them. 'That'll be *G-A-R-D . . .'*

'Wait a minute. That's *G-U-A-R-D.'*

'Now, why should there be a *U* there? No, don't tell me, it just *is*, is that right?'

'Yes,' said Debra, smiling back at him. 'It just *is*.'

15

There were to be no more names handed out. Cal decided this a few days later, when he heard the details of the Shon and Maxon business. Other odd things had been happening too: Jan, who had a crush on Peto, got hold of a copy of his name and wore it round her neck. When Peto found out, he was angry. In a fit of pique, Jan tried to throw the wooden label into the fire, and then Peto got angrier, and frightened too, almost as though it were himself who was being burned. Somebody was making copies of Cal's name, and selling them as a protection against fever. Someone else climbed a tree to cut branches without the safety harness he should have worn. 'It's all right,' he assured them, 'I'm wearing my name.' Debra was shocked by all this. She tried to explain, but nobody would listen.

Still, the days slipped by fast, so fast that she began to lose track of how long she had been there. It felt like forever, and she was beginning to forget that there had ever been another world in her life. The highlight of each day was the lesson with Cal. He was learning fast, though it would be a long time before he was a fluent reader. The hour or so each day that she spent with Cal almost blotted out all the other things like the poor food, the smells, Annet's continuing hostility. She forgot that the first time she met Cal, she had seen only a small man who had looked a little like a smiling bird; now he filled so much of her mind that she had no place for anything else.

She made one discovery that pleased her when she asked Palmer one day why Annet was so unfriendly to her.

'It's a bit hard for her,' he said, 'being Cal's sister.'

His sister! She wanted to laugh out loud. And she had thought that Annet was her rival. Well, Cal liked her, and if that didn't please Annet, it was just too bad. Anyway, Annet seemed to be avoiding her now, which suited Debra. With most of the others, especially Mara, Jan and Palmer, she got on very well.

It wasn't Palmer, though, who first told her of the plan to get the books from the Poison Tower. Peto mentioned it one day when he was showing her the results of his latest attempts at paper-making. So far, this was not proving very successful, and he had produced only a small thick fibrous mat, far too stiff and absorbent to be of any use. But he was going to carry on, and now talked of adding other things, like rags and plant fibre to his mixture, and perhaps mixing in glue, or size. 'Once I've seen some real paper,' he said, 'I can try to work out how they did it.' This led on to the plan. Cal's people had recently recruited a man who worked as a cleaner in one of the guards' barracks, and this man had got hold of, and copied, a set of keys to the Poison Tower. Cal was now working on a scheme to get one of his people inside the tower.

Like most things in the Hidden House, this happened covertly at first, and then was suddenly everywhere. One moment, it was only a rumour, the next everyone was telling you the details and how it was to be carried out.

Palmer was to be the person to enter the Tower. He would go there at night; the area round the Tower was regularly patrolled, but there was a clear period of half an hour, during which he could enter and bring away whatever he could find. The plan seemed most simple, and Debra wondered why it had never been attempted before. But, of course, before they had no-one to help them make sense of the books.

'Don't you have any idea at all what's in there?' she said to Cal during that afternoon's lesson. He was concentrating hard. They were on the letter *K*, and the words Cal wanted to make, *King*, and *Kingdom* seemed part of his preoccupation. 'None at all,' he said. '*D-U-M*?'

'*D-O-M*. It's the same as in *FREEDOM* and *WIS-DOM*.'

'Freedom, and wisdom,' he said, thoughtfully. 'Well, when we have one, we will have both, I hope, though who's to say which will come first? Now – *CROWN*. Is that a *k* or a *c*?'

'It's *c*. How will Palmer know what to bring back?'

'He won't. He must hazard a guess, and bring what he can.'

'If I went with him, I might be able to choose the books you want.'

He gave her a strange look. 'So you might, my dear. But I shan't send you.'

'Why not?'

'Not this time. *CONSPIRACY* – how does that start?'

Palmer would leave at midnight, and would take one companion with him, to keep a lookout for the patrols, and to flash a signal up at the Tower when all was clear. As usual, when something was happening, nobody had much time for Debra, and she had learned to fade into the background.

The hours passed; shortly before midnight, Palmer left, with Maxon, who was to be his companion. The little juggler was solemn and abstracted; for once there were no jokes and no wisecracks as he set off into the darkness.

Debra did not intend to sleep for very long while he was away, but having tossed restlessly on her mattress for a while, she fell fast asleep, to be woken up, she did not know how much later, by Mara, pulling at her. 'Quickly, Debra. Come and see.'

It was just beginning to get light as Debra stumbled out of bed. Outside the window, the sky was grey and grainy. The air was cold and tasted of fog. She pulled a shawl around her and hurried to the ballroom where everyone had gathered.

In spite of the early hour, a celebration was going on. The morning light came mistily through tarnished windows, settling on the faded ornate woodwork. An oil-lamp had been lit, and made a little island of joyous light with, for once, no-one worrying whether it might be seen. There was Cal, laughing, one arm flung round Palmer's shoulder. And there was Palmer, laughing too, but nervously. As Debra approached, she could hear him describing events from his expedition. 'I thought they'd seen me then; this is it, I thought, and I waited. But no, on they went, tramp, tramp, tramp, and I was all right . . . Then. . . .'

His face was pale in the light, and a little shiny with sweat, but it was not to be wondered at after such a perilous night.

As Debra approached, everyone fell silent. Then they all started clamouring at once. 'He's got the books!'

Cal left Palmer, and came over to her. His bird-like face was full of excitement, half suppressed, as he always suppressed any of the more unruly emotions.

'Well?' she said.

'Well?' he said, laughing. Then he turned and clapped his hands. 'Go on, all of you. Take Palmer for some breakfast and the rest of you get some sleep.'

It took some minutes for everyone, overcharged as they were with excitement, to obey him, and leave the ballroom. Eventually they all went, Palmer, Annet, Shon, Maxon, Jan, Lin, Peto.

She was alone with Cal in the high room.

And it was only then that she saw what lay on the floor, wrapped up in a large sheet of oilcloth.

'The books!' she said. 'You've got them!'

16

'I haven't even looked at them myself yet,' Cal said. 'Palmer said they were very fragile; they were disintegrating in his hands.'

Cal knelt down and, carefully and delicately, began to unwrap the oilcloth bundle. There were four large identical volumes, bound in faded red cloth, the binding worn to shreds on the spines and corners. As he picked up a book, a shower of brittle yellow fragments fluttered to the floor, and Debra picked one up. The paper almost crumbled to dust in her hands, but she was able to read the tiny print.

> TAYLOR, J. H, 32, Hornsey Drive
> TAYLOR, J. C, 61, Wellington H
> TAYLOR, John C, 199, Argyll
> TAYLOR, J. D, 3/67 Gibson
> TAYLOR, J. D, 14, Spen
> TAYLOR, J. D, 301 Wil
>   YLOR, J. D, 4, Po
>   OR, J. D, 18,
>   R, Joh

At first it did not make any sense, and then suddenly it did. She felt a constriction in her throat. 'But Cal, these are . . .'

Cal turned the top volume over. 'There's a label here.'

'But, Cal . . .'

He had not heard. 'S-Z. The . . . Lon . . . the London – Debra, look, the name of your city – the London T . . . Tel . . .'

She had to take over. '*The London Telephone Directory, 1970. Volume Four. The Twentieth Century Archive Collection* . . .'

And she knew perfectly well what would be written on the other three . . .

A-D, E-K, L-R.

Cal saw the disappointment on her face. He sat back on his heels and waited for her to speak, not urging her as most other people would have done, letting her take time to find her words.

Which were not easy to choose. In the end she said, 'Cal, these books are no use to you.'

She tried to explain, though in her explanation, she had to describe telephones, something she had not mentioned to them so far. 'Somebody must have thought things like this worth collecting. But it's only a list of names and addresses.'

He laughed, or tried to laugh. 'Palmer said, there was a room full of books. He couldn't carry them all, so he chose the biggest.'

'I'm sorry.'

'I had hoped for a history. Or even a book of science. Or one of the great writers you tell me about.'

He looked at the faded red cover for some time. Then when he spoke again, it was almost as though he had got over the disappointment. 'You say that word is *telephone*,' he said thoughtfully. 'Are you telling me that *ph* says *f*?'

Later that evening, Palmer, fed and rested, told his

story, as everyone sat around the long table by the extravagant light of several candles and an oil-lamp. His face was still pale and there were beads of sweat around his mouth; but this was probably because he was still in a state of high excitement.

'So there we were,' he said, 'me and old Mac, waiting in the darkness, while round and round they went, left right, left right, left right. When the coast was clear, Mac and I looks at each other. "This is it?" I says. "This is it," he says. So there am I, creeping across the square, with this big shiny moon looking down on me. "Well, whose side are you on," I want to say. I can see it, all glittering. I think, how pretty it looks, that green spire.

'Anyway, I'm not there to think how pretty, am I? So I get to the door, and out comes my key. It isn't a big door, not for somewhere so important. Funny, really. Anyway, in goes the old key, and hey presto, it turns like a knife in butter. Lovely. Inside, it's dark, and I don't want to light my candle, so I have to grope a bit. There's a kind of narrow stairway, that goes round and up. It's quite easy to climb, once you get the hang of it. There isn't a scrap of light, as I say. And I don't know how long it is since anyone was last there; it smells like a bloody graveyard. Anyway, I go up and up, and try not to think about it. Then suddenly I'm in front of another door. "Well this is it," I think, and in I go. Well, I get the shock of my life, don't I? I'm expecting a room full of books, and this is empty. Only it isn't dark. It's all lit up, that's the strange thing. All round the walls, these little niches, and these strange lights, glowing away. I've never seen anything like them; they were lovely. A sort of blue-ish glow. At first I don't know what to think, it's so pretty, but where are the books? Then I see another door. More stairs . . .'

Here the little man suddenly stopped. He had become

quite out of breath in his excitement. Somebody said, 'Are you all right?' and he nodded, took a few swigs of beer, and was able to carry on.

'Up I go. Then another door. I go in. This time, there isn't a light, so I have to light my candle, and hope no-one sees outside. And at last, here I am. I think, this is it! If only Cal was here to see this. Books everywhere, all round the walls, hundreds of them, all in rows on shelves. I don't know where to start . . .'

Cal smiled at Debra across the table. It had been difficult to make Palmer understand about the telephone directories, so full was he of himself, and his cleverness in having chosen only the largest books.

Cal got quietly to his feet, and gestured to Debra to follow. They slipped away from the table, without anyone seeming to notice.

'It's hot in here,' he said. 'I thought I'd go for a walk outside. Coming?'

Debra nodded, and followed him through the maze of stairways and corridors. He took her through a door she did not know, out onto a balcony. 'Don't lean on the wall,' he said. 'It's crumbling away.' She saw fallen pillars, and a statue, on the ground, smashed in two, which still raised a handless arm to the night sky. Beyond, a flight of wide steps led down, and suddenly stopped in mid-air, beckoning perilously to a terrace that no longer existed. And in the distance the jumbled roofs and spires of the city, everything in darkness, except for here and there, a sprinkle of lights. 'It's beautiful,' she said, and Cal laughed.

'Are they all like you, where you come from,' he said, 'with a taste for ruins and broken down places? We shall sweep all this away one day, and have a clean new city, with lights in the streets, and people walking confidently about.'

She had to laugh at herself, and admit that it was silly of her to find such things beautiful. They weren't, of course, beautiful if you had to live in them. Cal's clean new city must be a better place than the old. And she didn't doubt that one day, it would exist.

But it seemed that Cal didn't for the moment want to talk about the new city. 'Poor Palmer,' he said. 'I couldn't listen to him being so happy.'

'But it wasn't a complete waste,' Debra said. 'At least now you know how to get in the Tower.'

'Palmer was lucky this time; another time he might not be.'

'I wonder what all those books were.'

'Everything we could want, I expect, if only we could get at them.'

'Cal, why don't you let me go to the Tower? I can read the books, and only choose the useful ones.'

He looked down at her in the darkness. She could see his face pale as marble, like something sculpted. 'It might be dangerous, you know.'

'I don't mind that.' And as she said it, it was true.

'I'm not sure,' he said. 'We can't hazard you. You're too important to us.'

She glowed with pride. If only the others were here, if only Annet had heard him say that!

She could not resist trying to fish for further compliments. 'Am I?' she said.

And for once in her life, vanity was rewarded. He put a hand on her shoulder. 'Of course you are,' he said. 'Since you came, things have altered completely. You've been very special for us, Debra. You know that.'

* * *

You've been very special for us, Debra, very special, very special. . . . She went over and over these words in her head. He had really said them to her! It was like a magic food that could sustain her for weeks. *Very special.* She had not imagined them. For a few days she went round in a trance, hardly noticing what went on about her. In fact, things seemed to have fallen quiet. Palmer was not very well and stayed in his room. Everybody in the City, Mara said, was prone to recurring bouts of what they called Sweat Fever. Debra wondered if it was malaria, and hoped she wouldn't fall prey to it herself. Lessons with Cal continued as usual, and they even found the pages at the start of the telephone directories quite useful as an example of text, though it gave them a strange set of vocabulary: 'How to Call the Operator,' 'Emergency Services,' 'Directory Enquiries,' but Cal found it amusing. 'If the instrument is out of order . . .' he would say, and laugh. His reading was progressing fast now; if only they had had some real books.

But somehow, over the next days, she found that her suggestion was beginning to turn into reality. Cal began by saying to her, 'If you were to go to the Tower,' but soon it was 'When you go to the Tower.'

Who was to go with her? Not Palmer, certainly. His Sweat Fever was too bad, just at present. Maxon might accompany her, as he had gone with Palmer, though he would wait outside. By imperceptible stages, the thing progressed from being an idea in the air, to a definite plan, with a date and a time. Now the date was the following day, the time just after midnight. Although it was supposed to be secret, most people now knew that she was going. She found herself talking about it with Mara in the kitchen. 'I'm really excited,' she said. 'I've never done anything dangerous before. I hope I don't let you down. Of course, as Palmer says, it's simply a matter of timing, getting the timing right, so you don't bump into the patrol . . .'

'These carrots are rotten,' Mara said. 'I don't know how they expect me to cook them. Look at them. And they cost so much, too.'

Well, perhaps you could understand Mara not wanting to talk about it. After all, she was one of those who had to stay behind and wait, while Debra had all the glory.

The only person who did seem to want to talk was Annet, surprisingly. 'What's this crazy idea?' was what she said to Debra. 'Why are you doing this?'

'Because Cal thinks it's a good idea,' Debra said, hoping to silence her.

'Why must you interfere in our affairs?' Annet said. 'You don't know what you're doing, do you? You should go back to your own place. I told you, you don't understand us, you'll never understand us.'

'I understand some things when I see them,' Debra retorted. 'Jealousy, for example. You've never liked me, have you? You want to spoil everything for me!'

'Oh, have it your own way, you stupid girl,' snapped Annet. The two girls glowered at each other. But then, Cal entered the room, and both turned away, ashamed but silently fuming.

17

Debra vaguely noticed people coming and going, whispering around the stairway that led to the upper rooms, but her mind was too full to pay much heed to them. She began to prepare for her mission as soon as it grew dark, dressing in the same black shapeless clothes she had worn when she came to the City at night, and for the same reason – not to be seen. It was strange to be in her old London clothes again; for some time now she had worn a long green City dress which Mara had found for her.

And over and over again, she rehearsed the plan. Maxon would see her safely through the City, by the labyrinth of paths well known to Cal's people, dodging the patrols. They would wait in the shadows near the Poison Tower and he would tell her when it was safe to cross the square and enter. From then on it was up to her. First, there would be the main door, opened with the biggest of the keys – and Palmer had said it opened easily. The dark stairway frightened her a little – oh, for a London torch with a battery! But it would soon be over, and then there was the door which led to the mysteriously lit ante-room. Another door, a stair, and another, and she would be in the chamber of the books. She would light the candle which she had hidden under her cloak, with the cumbrous flint which was the City equivalent of matches, and then there was half an hour for her search. The candle, which was ringed, would also act as a timer: when one ring had burned through, it would be time to leave, first looking through the window for Maxon's signal.

She thought, if I do this, it will be the first worthwhile thing I have ever done in my life. I'll show that I can be brave, and it'll be something that no-one else in the City, not even Cal, can do. She was scared, of course, in fact she was so nervous thinking about it, she could hardly breathe, but that wasn't important. What was important was not to let Cal down.

And what were the books she would find? She had talked about it with Cal. Most of all, he wanted something that would repair the distorted picture they had of their own history in the City; he was sure that such a book existed. There were many other gaps to be filled, in science and technology. It was an impossible task, really, for one journey to accomplish everything. 'But I can always go a second time,' Debra said eagerly to Cal. He did not seem to think this was a good idea. 'We need to lessen the risks, Debra. So bring as much as you can this time.'

The night passed. So slowly at first that it seemed she would be in a state of expectancy for ever, and then suddenly, all in a rush, it was time. Maxon was there, also dressed in black; he carried the things she would need, the keys, her candle and flint, a sack to carry the books. Not many people were there to see her off, but Cal was there, and that was all that mattered. He walked with them to the street door, and then, before Maxon had opened the door, he put his arms around her, and kissed her on the forehead. 'Goodbye, Debra,' was all he said, and she could not manage even a word in reply.

Outside, the night was dark and cold, with the tang of smoke on the air, but for a while Debra, remembering that he had kissed her, noticed nothing. Maxon walked in front; she followed, in and out of doorways, through passages, down steps. They passed through the Old Work, into the centre of the City, sometimes waiting in the shadows while a patrol marched past.

They emerged into one of the streets she knew, a street of arches and colonnades. It was strange to be back in the heart of her City; she had missed it during the time spent in the Hidden House. There was very little moonlight that night, and she could see only outlines, the solidity of buildings, the curve of arches, the faintest sheen of light on stone. She remembered the smell though, rotting vegetation and mould, but also a faint scent on the air that was none of these; the smell of the City itself. One day, they would build a bright new City, Cal had said, and of course that was right; this was a bad place, and it would have to go, but it was beautiful too.

'We've got to get over there,' hissed Maxon in her ear, 'but be careful, this street is patrolled all the time. See that second archway, the one below that window? Well, when I say go, you cross the road and wait for me there. I'll see the coast's clear and then I'll come too. I'll only be a minute or so behind you. All right?'

'All right,' Debra whispered, and at his signal, she darted out, into the dark road, and across the other side. Beyond the archway, she could see nothing but blackness. She pulled her coat around her, and entered.

The darkness was stifling, it caught in her throat like fog, and seemed to wrap round her tight as bonds. Something impelled her forward, as though she was being pushed into it, as though she was being forced into a vacuum. She could not breathe.

Lights danced and dazzled somewhere in front of her, her ears filled with noise . . .

18

There were not many people around at that time in Holland Park. A grey track-suited jogger had just passed by, sweatily panting. A middle-aged man whose intentions were almost certainly dishonourable hovered around the sandpits where a few brave nannies shivered as their charges played. A park-keeper prodded bits of litter with his spiked stick. The sky was silvery cold; last night's frost had rimed the spiky leaves that still fringed the pond, the bare trees were fixed and rigid in the wintery air. A mother, red-nosed with the cold, pushed her baby in a double pushchair, while her older child, wrapped in a red and yellow scarf, bounded happily along, the brightest and liveliest thing to be seen in the chill park.

The child stopped running and singing, and stared in astonishment, at the dishevelled girl in black, blundering along the path, crying and calling out. The girl beat her fists helplessly against the wall, shouting, in a strange high-pitched voice, 'Let me back, let me back!'

'Mummy,' said the child very clearly, 'is that lady drunk?' Mummy, though, who had had enough loonies for today, thank you very much, hardly turned to look. 'Come along, Rebecca,' she said listlessly. 'Just get in that pushchair, will you?' The child obeyed, though still swivelling round to watch the mad lady with interest. In a minute she remembered that the sweet shop was just round the corner and changed her cry. 'Mummy, can I have an ice-cream, can I?'

That clear loud voice, though, penetrated Debra's consciousness as nothing else had done. *'Is that lady drunk?'* She tried to pull herself together, and succeeded to a certain degree; at least she stopped shouting and hitting the wall.

There was no door back, she could not go back.

She knew that by instinct, yet she would not believe it. Whatever it was had taken her up by force, gobbled her in, and cast her out again, far from where she wanted to be. Her City, where she had been but a moment ago, was in a moment, gone, unreachable!

Some part of her brain registered that she was in Holland Park, and propelled her towards the exit. But the rest of her was somewhere else, in limbo, between worlds. To anyone that watched, she probably still looked drunk.

Why, oh why, why just at *that* moment, of all moments!

How noisy, how huge London was. Lorries of terrifying size lurched past. Cars flashed by at impossible speed. Buses were monsters, traffic lights flashed signals she had quite forgotten. She was hooted, shouted at. Crossing the huge roads full of speeding traffic was unmanageable. She tried to step out into the middle of it at one point, having quite forgotten about zebra crossings. Signs flashed and screamed at her from everywhere, STOP, GIVE WAY, HOTEL, KENTUCKY FRIED, LATE NITE; words, words, words; did people notice the words all around them?

And how oddly they spoke; voices grated on her ear like a badly tuned radio.

Here was – what was it called? The name came back to her from a place deep in her brain. Shepherd's Bush. Other names, Notting Hill, White City, Holland Park. The world that had been thrown up to the air in fragments now began to settle itself around her ears.

Inside the flat, something was making a terrible noise. She heard it for a while, without realising that it was a telephone. Telephones needed answering.

'Hallo?'

'Debra, where have you been? I've been calling for ages.'

Oh.

A familiar voice. Soon it registered.

Mum.

'Sorry – I – er . . .'

'Debra, are you all right?'

'No. I mean yes. I think . . . I think I've got a touch of flu.'

'I don't suppose you've been looking after yourself, have you?' A stream of maternal solicitudes flowed over her, late nights, not eating properly. She pulled herself somehow together. 'Mum, I'm all right, really I am.'

'. . . all this time . . .'

What time was it? What day?

'Did you hear what I just said?'

'Yes, Mum. I mean, what . . .'

'Debra, are you sure you're all right? You haven't been . . . drinking or anything, have you?'

Mummy, is that lady drunk?

'No, of course not. I said, just a bit of flu. I think I'll go to bed, actually.'

'So I'll be back on Friday then, did you hear me?'

'Yes, I heard.'

'Pardon?'

'That'll be great, Mum. Really great. I'm really looking forward . . . yes, really . . . no, of course not . . . Bye, Mum.'

At least the phone call had the effect of concentrating her mind. By the time she put the receiver down, she was, at last, in London, 1980s. She was home. Aspen Towers, Orchard Estate.

But what day? What time?

The evening newspaper lay on the sofa where she had left it last. Monday, November 20th.

She switched the television on, and watched the end of the children's programme. Then the announcer said: 'Good evening. Here is the six o'clock news for Tuesday, November 21st.'

For the rest of that evening, nothing was real. What was real was Maxon, waiting in the shadows for her, wondering what had become of her; Cal, and the kiss he had left on her forehead; Mara, and Jan, and Palmer. It was even Annet's angry little face screwed up close to hers.

Here water flowed hot from taps, lights came on when you pressed a switch, books and magazines were scattered in reckless profusion, voices came at you from machines. It was like a dream.

She had a hot bath later on: it was the one thing she had really missed in the City, where she had to get used to washing from ewers of cold water. And often, like everyone else, not bothering. Her clothes smelled of the City, musty and damp; she pressed them to her nose, as though by inhaling its smell, she could bring the City back.

100

They would be thinking she had deserted them!

If only she could have got a message to someone, if she could have predicted her return, if she had at least been to the tower and found the books first! She could imagine Annet saying gleefully, 'See, I told you all along she couldn't be trusted.' And Cal saying . . . what would he say? No, she could not think of it.

In the morning, everything was unreal still. She did not sleep anyway, her body operating on a different time clock. She remembered school, then the strike. So much had happened, and yet barely a day had passed.

Reality began to return after a fashion the following day. A news report – she watched the news to re-orient herself – said that the strike had after all been resolved. So she went to school, remembering Matthew on the way, and how once she had cared about meeting him.

She took the route through the Shepherd's Bush subway, through Holland Park, all the places where she'd found doors. Needless to say, there were none.

At school, she hurried to her form-room. Most people were already there, waiting for Miss Lovelace. Debra sat at her desk. She noticed that Julie Bexley was staring at her oddly. Debra opened a book, and studied it determinedly, but Julie came over.

'Hey, Debra, have you been on a diet?'

'What?' She looked up. Julie seemed friendly enough.

'Well, I just noticed.'

'What did you notice?'

'How much thinner you've got.'

'Have I?'

'Funny, I never noticed before. You must have been dieting for ages.'

Debra looked down at her wrists. There did seem to

be more bone poking through than was usual.

'Really amazing,' Julie went on. 'You must tell me how you did it. Hey,' she called to Sarah Evans. 'Come here. Hasn't Debra got thin?'

Sarah had a look too. 'Wow,' was what she said.

'Go on, Debra, tell us how you did it.'

'Well, nothing really.'

'Go *on*.'

'No, really. I guess I just haven't been hungry lately.'

'And there's something the matter with your voice. Have you got a cold, or something?'

No, thought Debra, what she did have was a City accent. All those weeks and she must have picked it up. Well, now she'd have to lose it again. 'I did have a bit of a sore throat,' she said in explanation.

Sarah nodded sagely. 'So's my mum. There's a lot of it around, you know.'

School proved to be a good thing. Perhaps because of the strike, there was a slightly wild spirit in the air as though it were a holiday, which meant no-one made any demands on Debra. She sat quietly at her desk, trying to come back to earth, and yet at the same time thinking desperately of the City and everyone there.

The City was where she wanted to be. Nothing could distract her from that.

The following day, there was the flat to be got ready for her mother. Things were not really untidy, but she had scattered papers and coffee cups everywhere. It was important to appear as normal and together as possible. If Mum sensed anything wrong, she would worry at it like a dog with a bone. And since she could not be told the truth she would, of course, imagine the worst. One thing was true, though. Like Julie had said, Debra had lost weight. Over a stone, in fact. She weighed herself that evening. One good thing to come from all that porridge and those bean stews. Of course, Mum would think she was ill, knowing her. So for the sake of pride, and family peace, Debra must put on a good front.

This too, was all for the best, and gradually she began to focus her mind on what was going on around her. By the time her mother was due to come back, the flat at least looked normal, and Debra practised her smile in front of a mirror.

19

Absence alters your memory of people, Debra found. Angry with her mother for going away, she had only remembered the negative things, arguments, injustices, shortcomings, so that her mother became almost an enemy in her mind. It was easy to forget the good things about her. And Debra had been away from her mother for a long time; much longer than her mother had been away from Debra, as it happened.

But the person who returned from Ireland was a sadder and more vulnerable one than Debra had seen in her darker moments. Subdued by the funeral, she was in no mood to pry and search, so that if there was anything different in Debra apart from her thinness, she did not seem to notice.

So there was Christmas, and Christmas too turned out better than it might have done. Debra bought a tree and decorated it in silver and green; they had a very small turkey and a bought Christmas pudding, and after Christmas dinner, Debra's mother had a little weep, thinking about her own childhood Christmases. The result of this was that they finished the day on better terms than they had been for some time.

There was school work to catch up with too, since she had missed so much.

And before the end of term, a conversation with Miss Lovelace gave her plenty to think about.

'Debra, have you started to plan what you're going to do in the sixth form yet?'

'The sixth form? No.'

'Then isn't it time you should? Mmn?'

'Is it?'

'Come, come, Debra. I thought you had your head screwed on better than that. You should be thinking about your Oxbridge entrance.'

'Oxbridge?'

'Yes, dear. It's what we call Oxford and Cambridge.'

Debra thought, if you think I'm so thick that you have to explain that, then why are we talking about this?

But all she said, politely, was, 'Do you think I stand a chance?'

'I should think you stand a very good chance. I think you'd be foolish not to try.'

But while Debra was digesting this, Miss Lovelace nearly spoiled everything by adding sharply, 'You're just the sort of person they're looking for at the moment. They're trying to bring in more children from disadvantaged backgrounds these days.'

And as Debra's mouth fell open, she turned and tap-tapped away on her smart shoes.

But the idea had been planted, even if only by Miss Lovelace, and would not be dislodged. Supposing she could get a scholarship to Oxford or Cambridge! What better way out of the Orchard Estate? Wherever she lived afterwards, it could be somewhere of her choosing, in a system in which she had some power. She might end up a lawyer, or a politician, or she might end up nothing at all. But at least she would have some control of her life.

Over Christmas, she mentioned the idea to her mother

who, to her surprise, didn't raise all the objections instantly, but merely said: 'Do your teachers think you could do that? It would be very nice, wouldn't it?'

But if she was thinking about Oxford and Cambridge, then that meant she could not think about the City.

And if she did not think about the City, then there was no Cal either.

She could not have both.

So which was it to be?

'Debra! You're looking very slim and glamorous!'

Matthew had come up on her without her seeing. She turned to see his bleached bottle-brush hair and battered grin. She started and blushed, and spoke crossly to cover up her confusion. 'You mean you're not ashamed to be seen talking to me any more?'

It wasn't quite what she'd meant to say. He'd been smiling, and then he was not. 'Still the same old Deb,' he said ruefully.

He was wearing new clothes from top to toe; new bomber jacket, new sweatshirt, new trousers and sneakers. If you didn't know, you'd think they were rubbish, but Debra caught the whiff of American designer labels.

'You look expensive,' was all she said.

'Did you have a nice Christmas, Matthew?' he said. 'Why, yes, thank you very much, and you, Debra, did you have a nice Christmas too?'

She managed the smile she should have found at first. 'Sorry. Did you?'

'Yes,' he said. 'Much to my surprise, I did. It was great. What about you?'

'Oh.' She found that she had hoped he would say that he had a lousy time. 'Yes, it was all right.' But how could an all right Christmas with mum and a small turkey compete with a great Christmas in Los Angeles and a millionaire dad?

'You seem different, Debra. Has anything happened?'

'Only the amazing weight loss that everyone keeps telling me about.'

'No, it's not just that. Something else.'

'What, for example?'

'Dunno. Just different.'

Matthew seemed different, too. He looked and sounded younger and brasher than she'd remembered him. But perhaps that was not his fault; after all, she was comparing him with someone older, someone with weightier things on his mind than buying designer clothes in Los Angeles.

She still searched for the door that would take her back to him.

But there were no doors.

And she would have felt bad, leaving at the moment, with Mum being so low. In the City, it was different; then she could contemplate almost without a pang never going back to London; when the City was all around her, it absorbed her utterly. But now she thought about what would happen if she went missing, the speculations, the searches, the grief. And the City began inevitably to recede, although she hated to think of this happening. The two worlds could not survive with equal weight in her mind; the one in which she was present inevitably dislodged the other.

She did not see Matthew to speak to again for several days. School exams were upon her, and this year she was determined to do well. And with all the giggling and gossiping that would ensue if they were seen too much in each other's company, they did not communicate very much at school. They arranged to meet though, one evening at a café on Shepherd's Bush Green.

He was back home with his mother now. Yes, she was better, he said, but in such a way as to convey that he did not really want to discuss her. He was much happier to talk about Christmas in Los Angeles. Dad and Venetia had been off partying most of the time, and he had seen very little of them. He'd got in with this crowd of wild Hollywood kids, most of them children of people in the movies. They all had cars and apparently limitless supplies of money. There was Mark, Jason, Karen, Duane, Jennifer, Lorri-Anne. Lorri-Anne drove her own 1958 Cadillac convertible. Debra couldn't help noticing that her name came up rather a lot in the conversation. 'So we all piled in, and went over to Lorri-Anne's.' 'Lorri-Anne said, "Jeez, my dad'll kill me if the cops catch us."' 'Lorri-Anne wanted burgers, so . . .' There might have been nothing in it, but Debra thought she noticed a slight catch in his voice when he mentioned her name. As though he wanted to drop it in the conversation as much as possible but felt uncomfortable doing so. After a while, Debra said grumpily, 'Lorri-Anne, what sort of a name is that?'

Matthew gave a great hoot of laughter, and said in his old way, 'Well, that's great, that is, coming from a girl whose name is Debra spelt funny.' That for the time being was that. They changed the subject, and spent a pleasantly bitchy half hour discussing the possibilities of Miss Lovelace's sex life.

20

The snow came in January, a fine, glittering layer of it, turning the Orchard Estate chill grey and chill white, an Arctic sea of great marooned icebergs. The piled snow quickly became mottled with grime, rubbish collected, frozen stiff like junk sculpture; people moved slowly and awkwardly, muffled out of recognition. Debra's mother was still worried about her dead sister's family left behind in Ireland; the grandmother was ill, and it seemed she would have to return for a few more days. Debra did well in all her exams except Physics – much, it seemed, to the irritation of everyone else in her class. Exams were not things to do well in. She had achieved a brief moment of social acceptability by losing weight, but now she was back in her old position as class freak.

Or perhaps she was being over-sensitive. Maybe that too accounted for the feeling of constraint she felt between herself and Matthew. They had not seen very much of each other, and school was so noisy and active that there were few chances of a quiet meeting.

They did bump into each other one morning in an empty corridor. It was the day that Debra's mother was due to go back to Dublin, though this time she intended to be back by the week-end. 'I can't face that bloody dining hall,' Matthew said. 'Let's go into the park and

109

have a sandwich there.'

In the park the snow was now trodden and dirty, a sea of footprints swirling round the field, and half-finished snowmen. The snow was no longer soft, but iced and grainy, though the temperature was still too cold for it to melt.

'This time a month ago,' Matthew said longingly, 'I was sitting by the pool.'

Debra remembered too what she had been doing a month ago. It was hard to even imagine what Cal might be doing now; she did not even know the dimension in which he existed. By comparison, Los Angeles might have been just around the corner.

The café was half empty. Matthew bought tomato soup and cheese rolls. 'God, I hate this weather,' he said. 'You think it's never going to be summer again.'

'I quite like the winter, really,' Debra said. 'It's just that it goes on for so long.'

'Trust you to be different from everyone else.'

'I just don't like all that sunbathing stuff. It's boring.'

'It's great,' Matthew said wistfully. 'Lying on a towel, nothing to do, good sounds on your Walkman, and an enormous iced coke.'

And Lorri-Anne, no doubt, in an almost non-existent bikini, Debra thought but did not say.

'Yes,' he went on, 'they don't know how lucky they are, those kids. They've got everything. But they're always moaning, you know.'

'What do they moan about?'

'Oh, everything, life, money, their parents. Mind, some of those parents are pretty screwed up. They make my mum and dad seem like the Cosby Show.'

'Do they?'

'You can't blame the kids really when they go off the rails.'

'I thought you had a great time.'

Matthew took a large bite of cheese roll. 'I did. But like I said, it was really wild, some of the things they did.'

'What, you mean like drugs and stuff?'

'Everything.'

A mad lady had come into the café, and sat at a table talking loudly to herself. She was wrapped up in at least one coat and several scarves. Her face was red and weatherbeaten as though she lived out in the cold. The few people in the café shifted uncomfortably as she ranted. 'They can't tell me, bloody tyrants they think they are, telling me what to do, well, I don't listen, do I, I don't care for their bloody rooms, stuff you full of bloody poison, they will . . .'

The rantings became obscene. An elderly lady with a dog tutted and left pointedly, muttering that really somebody somewhere should. Matthew grinned at Debra. 'Hey, I reckon I'll end up like that one day.'

'No you won't,' Debra said. But it made her uncomfortable. Mad people had the same sorrows and grievances as everyone else, only something went wrong with the way they processed them. Sometimes she felt that the border between the mad and the sane was dangerously fragile.

The woman was beginning to shout now, accusing everyone of trying to kill her. The waitresses were looking peeved, when quite abruptly, she rose and left.

In the silence behind her, a few people laughed, and then a buzz of embarrassed, relieved conversation broke out. *'Should be in a home.' 'Well, some of them won't.' 'Shame, really.'*

It meant though, that Matthew and Debra had lost the

thread of their conversation. Debra tried to pick it up again, and plunged more clumsily into the subject than she'd meant to.

'Did she take drugs and things?'

'Who?'

'Lorri-Anne.'

He gave her an odd look across the table. 'Not the really bad stuff. But here and there, you know.'

'Was she pretty?'

'I guess. Want another cheese roll?'

'No, thanks.'

'Well, I do. I'm starving.'

She watched as he went over to the counter, in his baseball jacket and long scarf. The girl serving him was blonde and pretty, and something he said to her made her giggle as she passed his cheese roll across the counter.

'I don't know what's the matter with me,' he said, as he returned to the table and bit into it. 'I'm always hungry these days.'

And then his confidence seemed to return to him. 'Yes, she took me to this really wild party one day. Great big house in one of those canyons. The parents had gone away. But we had some great times.'

'Did you sleep with her?' Debra said.

Matthew stopped eating and looked at her. For a moment, everything in the café seemed to go as stiff and frozen as the park outside. The little waitress stood with her hand on her hip, another customer had his hand arrested half-way to his mouth with a coffee cup.

Debra wondered briefly if she had spoken too loudly, for she felt as if a stone had been dropped. But she had not. Only Matthew with his mouth hanging open had heard her.

'What did you say?'

'You heard.'

'Yes.'

'Yes what?'

'What do you mean?'

'Yes you heard or yes you slept with her?'

He tried to smile at her. 'Give us a break, Debra.'

'What's that supposed to mean?'

'Well, things are different out there. Nothing means the same.'

'So you did.'

'Look, Debra, it's not what you think. Don't be angry.'

'Oh, I'm not angry,' Debra said coldly.

He grinned. 'Yes, I can see that, Debra. It's really great, you not being angry.'

'It's no business of mine, what you do.'

'Isn't it?'

'*No!*'

For a few moments he ate his cheese roll in silence. Then he said, 'Besides, you can't talk.'

'What's that supposed to mean?'

'No . . . listen . . . hell, I don't mean that you . . . But you met somebody while I was away, didn't you?'

'No. Why?'

'It stands out a mile.'

'How can you say that?'

'I can tell. The same way you sussed out about me and Lorri-Anne.'

'Well, I didn't.'

'Suit yourself.'

'Just because . . . why do people always imagine that?'

'Because it's true. Look at you. You can say it isn't till you're blue in the face. We're neither of us great liars, Debra, more's the pity.'

'I'm not trying to lie. And you're just trying to change the subject, aren't you?'

'Probably.'

'Well, I'm not going to sit here . . . anyway, it's time to get back. I'm off. I'm going. You can do what you like.'

21

Returning that night with a splitting headache to an empty flat was almost like the time before Christmas. Mum had left her some money in a purse, a list of instructions and a chicken casserole.

She hadn't intended to be mad at Matthew. It was none of her business what he got up to. And she wasn't shocked in that sense. She was just . . .

Oh hell.

The other day, she was just beginning to feel that she was getting everything together at last, and now . . .

It was a fairly miserable evening she spent, watching all the junk on television.

The following day, at school, Matthew seemed quite definitely to be avoiding her. She hung around at lunch time, hoping to see him and perhaps apologise, but he did not come near.

All through the afternoon, she watched him across the classroom, hunched over his work. Then, between classes, he was sitting on his desk, amiably hurling insults at Steve and Leroy. He did not even look in her direction. You've certainly blown that one, Debra, she told herself. Well done.

When she talked to Cal, she could find the right words, without getting into muddles; it was as though she was saying directly what was in her soul.

But Cal was mature, he understood things, he knew what he was doing. There could be no comparison between him and Matthew.

To her embarrassment she found herself writing a name on her file: CAL. She was going to cross it out, but changed her mind. Leave it there. It could mean nothing to anybody here. Did not even sound like a name.

And writing it seemed to bring him closer.

It was dark that evening; a leaden sky promised more snow. As she stood by the school door, she saw lights coming on in the buildings around the park. Trees, stiff as brushes, were ranged around, blurring in the twilight. She set off feeling the cold air on her face, thrusting her hands – she had forgotten her gloves – as deep in her pockets as she could.

She thought for a moment she heard her name being called, but the sound was lost in the cold air, and she hurried on. But before she reached the park gates someone caught up with her.

It was Matthew. His face was glowing with the cold, and the breath puffed out in little clouds in front of him.

'You ignoring me, or something?' he said with an embarrassed smile.

'Don't be silly.'

'Look, I've got something for you.' He fished in his inside pocket and brought out a bulging envelope. 'It's got all squashed, I'm afraid.'

And, as she hesitated, 'Go on, it won't bite.'

'What is it?'

'It's . . . oh, read it and see. I thought, when I open my big mouth, I only put my foot in it. So last night, I wrote it all down. I don't know if it makes it any better.'

'I . . .'

'Don't read it now. It's all silly rubbish. But listen, do read it sometime, won't you?'

'Thanks,' she said. 'I will, Matthew.'

'Thanks,' he said. And in one of his silly voices, '*And ven you haf read it, you must destroy it, all right?*'

'All right,' she said, smiling at him. 'I'll tear it into little pieces and swallow them, right?'

'Right!' he said. And '*Right!*' And he was off, loping into the chill twilight.

She was already inside the park, so she continued in that direction, stuffing Matthew's letter carefully inside her pocket. Everything was monotone now, like an old sepia photograph, the snow against the bare trees. There were only a few people about, and the kiosk was just closing as she went past.

She kept close to the wall, in the hope that this might keep out the icy cold, but it did not. Really, she was out of her mind to come this way; she should have gone for the bus. She nearly slipped on a pile of snow, and staggered against the wall. As she did so, her hand felt something.

She was clasping a door handle. A door set among brickwork and dry vines.

She turned the handle.

At first there was just darkness and fog, and the feeling of not being able to breathe. But then there was a burst of light, and warmth. She almost fell out, into bright sunlight.

Into sunlight, and the stone polished bright as copper, sharp shadows making black diagonals in the road. The sky was clear and clean, and the curves and pinnacles of the roofs sparkled in the light. In the distance, the sun shone on the vivid green curlicues of the Poison Tower.

117

It was a road she knew well, the road where she had first seen Annet selling sausages, and first encountered the black-clad Guardians. But coming there now, in the fresh warm air, was enough to make her laugh out loud.

The road was almost empty. From the distance came the sound of hammering, and a man was pushing a handcart round the corner. A woman opened a window, shook out a dishcloth and shut it again. Debra found herself walking up the road, rashly, right in the middle. Too soon to be cautious, it was enough simply to celebrate being back.

Nothing appeared different in the City, and yet she felt a change. Perhaps it was the sunlight. There were pots on windowsills, burgeoning with flowers and herbs, and here and there were signs of fresh carpentry. Yet the stonework still crumbled, and the drains smelled bad.

Ahead of her, she could see the big square, with the fountain. There was the sound of wheels rumbling over cobbles, a dog barking, someone shouting out.

It was at the corner of the street, just where it joined the square that she noticed the first change. There just at the level of the first floor windows, above the arcade, was a sign.

It was of wood, painted white, picked out in black. And it said SUTHEN STREET.

It should have been Southern Street, of course. That was how they referred to one of the four streets that converged on the main square. The others were Northern, Eastern and Western Street, points of a compass no longer of use to them.

She crossed out into the square. In the distance, she could see the fantastic confectionery of the palace, where the God-King had once stepped onto the balcony, glittering bronze and gold. The windows were shuttered, and the huge steps were empty. Perhaps it was the afternoon siesta, for only a few people were visible. But there was something else, a white shape on the wall round the fountain.

She went over to it. A sheet of coarse, inferior, porous paper. It said, in crudely hand-printed letters:

MEETING
TO DISCUS THE
NU REGULASHONS FOR
SAFETY AT WERK.

TONITE AT 6.
BRED STREET MEETING HOUS
AL AR WELCUM

What was going on? She walked round the fountain. On the far side was another. This one said:

WORNING TO AL SITIZENS!
THER AR STIL ENIMYS
HOO WONT TO DISTROY
AL THAT WE HAV DUN.
REPORT AL SUSPISHOS ACTS
TO A LEEDER.

She reached out to touch the paper. As she did so, she heard a distant voice calling, 'Hey! You! Leave it alone!' and the sound of running footsteps. She froze, and turned to see the worst.

But the woman running towards her, pulling up her

long green dress, stopped about twenty yards away, and then Debra saw her smile.

'Debra! It's you! You've come back.'

And Debra recognised Mara, though a Mara who looked different, older. Her clothes, though in the usual City style, long loose dress and shawl, were smarter and finer, and there was a decorated silver buckle on her belt.

Mara embraced her and then stood back to look. 'You don't look any different. You haven't changed at all.'

Well, of course I haven't, thought Debra.

But Mara had changed. Her face was thinner, and the lines around her mouth when she smiled were deeper.

'And you just come out of nowhere, like you always did! After all this time!'

'Mara,' Debra said slowly, 'just how long have I been away?'

'Why, it must be two years, I suppose.'

'*Two years?*'

'Of course. It was before . . .' She stared at Debra again. 'Then you don't . . . you can't know . . .'

'What's been happening, Mara?'

Mara laughed. 'Why, everything! Oh, Debra, it's been . . . And you mean you don't know about it?'

'How could I? I've been away.'

'Well, you must hear! Oh, this is wonderful.'

Debra looked round the square. She saw that everywhere knots of curious people were watching her and Mara. 'Are we safe here?'

'Safe? Of course we're safe. Don't you know . . . no, of course you don't. Well, let's go into the Palace, and I'll tell you everything.'

'The Palace?'

'Yes, it's all ours now. All ours.'

'Then Cal . . . the God-King . . .'

'No, wait, I'll tell you everything. Though I hardly know where to start!'

22

Great doors opened and closed behind them; Mara in her green dress hurried along marble floors, through long corridors. 'We'll talk here.' She opened a door into a little room, all gilt and ornament. 'The God-King used to sit here, and now we use it.'

'Where's the God-King now?'

'They killed him, the Guardians, when we stormed the palace, so we wouldn't find out. But we found out all the same. He wasn't a God-King at all, you know, just an ordinary man, a petty thief called Black Joe. He disappeared in prison years ago.'

'I don't understand.'

'It was like Cal always told us; the God-King was an excuse; just someone to fill the robes. It was the Guardians who had all the power.'

'Yes, but . . .'

Mara laughed. 'Of course, I forget, you don't have any idea, do you? Everything happened so fast, you see.'

'Tell me.'

'Things were happening, even when you were here. Remember Evan, the man who died in prison? Well, more people were killed, and there were riots in the streets. So we began to organise people. Everyone hated the Guardians. We'd all lost somebody, every family in the City. Well, there was fighting. Months of it, when nothing seemed to go right. Those were terrible times. We lost lots of people. Lin was killed, you know, and Shon and Peto. So many people. But then gradually, we began to win. Cal knew exactly what had to be done. And then just over a year ago, we stormed the Palace. Some of the Guardians escaped, some were killed. We held trials in the square; we hanged them. Nobody was sorry. They were wicked men. And since that day . . .' She spread out her hands and smiled. 'It's as you can see.'

'But Cal . . . where is Cal?'

'He's here. He's here now. I expect he's working in his office. Everything has to be reorganised. He's our Leader. It's wonderful. At least it will be. We want to close down the Farms, for example, all those prisoners. But we can't at the moment, we need the food supplies. But Cal is planning everything.'

'So Cal is king now?'

Mara shook her head vigorously. 'No! No more kings, no more Gods, no more Guardians. Cal was quite clear about that. We're the provisional government, just until things get going. There are still enemies about. We must be on our guard.'

'I saw the sign in the square.'

'Yes! We have written signs now. That's all thanks to you.'

'Can people read them?'

'Cal is seeing to that. There are going to be classes . . . But look, I can't keep you all to myself. You must come and meet everyone . . .'

Debra's hand was shaken she did not know how many times. Men and girls in green uniforms, the soldiers of the new order, rushed up to her. Debra got the impression that nobody quite knew who she was, or where she had come from, but everyone was pleased to see her. All around her, she saw fresh, enthusiastic faces, bright-eyed. If Mara said she was a friend, that was enough. And there were some faces she recognised. Maxon was there, with a new scar on his cheek, and Hood and Liss and Mal, from the old days. Though it was hard to remember that two years and a revolution had passed since she had last seen them just before Christmas.

She was embraced warmly, and told again how she did not look a day older.

But still there was Cal.

'Can I see him?'

'He's in a meeting with the safety group; so many people are killed in accidents and fires; we have to do something about it. The Guardians never cared about that.'

'So when can I . . .'

'In a while, I expect. He knows you're here. Liss sent up a message.'

'Oh.' For she had hoped that he might have rushed to see her, just as she would have rushed to see him, but of course he was a busy man. Not just the leader of a band of outlaws any more, but somebody important.

That morning, they showed her the City. She saw the places where they would start schools, the hospitals. She saw the place where they were going to erect a monument to those who had died in the fighting. She went down the wide, colonnaded streets, and the narrow, crooked ones, no longer a fugitive, but an honoured visitor. People came to windows and doors to see her, and one woman pressed flowers into her arms. 'They don't know who I am,' she said to Mara, who was showing her round.

'But they can see you're important,' Mara said. 'That's all that matters.'

So at last, she could think of it as *her* City; could stand in its streets and its shadows, and feel that she had a part in it: no more keeping out of sight, no more evading pursuers. It was as if she had come home.

And she saw parts of the City that she had never seen before. As well as the wide, tranquil streets, there were noisy, squalid tenements, with whole families crammed into single rooms. In the old days, these people had to keep in their own area, so that the more fortunate citizens did not have to be aware of them. Soon, Mara said, the slums would be pulled down, and new houses built.

If things had not altogether changed overnight, there was a feeling that all would be different soon, and that was enough.

Someone was escorting her, a young, uniformed man she did not know, up the great sweeping stairway, and down a wide corridor. Dark polished wood gleamed everywhere, carved into heavy bulbous shapes. Great lamps of twisted gilt sent juddering shadows down the darkness, sinister glitterings on wood and stone. Carved statues and shapes loomed up at her, and there were signs of the fighting, the God-King's sunbursts defaced, walls scarred with smoke, or slashed with knives.

Before a huge pair of double doors, the wood polished almost black, the young man stopped, and saluted. Another guard came forward, and flung the doors open. Debra passed through.

He sat at a desk, wearing black, a pile of papers before him.

'So you turn up again,' he said, 'out of the blue.'

She grinned awkwardly, horribly aware of her awkwardness. 'Hallo, Cal.'

He did not rise from his desk, or embrace her, and she felt a little disappointed, but he was a busy man.

'Do you see what I'm doing?' he said. What he was doing was writing a sign, black paint on porous matted paper.

She bent over to look.

LERN TO REED.
CUM TO A MEETING AT . . .

'See what you taught me,' he said with some pride.

'I taught you better spelling than that,' she said and he laughed.

'You taught me your way of spelling. But your traditions aren't any use to us now. We have a new City. We want our own ways of doing things.'

'But it looks so peculiar, like that.'

'Only to you.'

'It's wrong.'

'Wrong is only what you say it is. My way makes more sense than yours. It would take years to teach all those peculiar words, *though*, and *once* and *knife*. We haven't the time.'

No, he was probably right. But it meant – it meant that she was no longer of any use to them.

'I've taught a few people the rudiments of reading,' he said. 'Annet knows, but she's too busy at the moment working in the hospital. But there's a little group, who are going to pass it on.'

'I could help you do that.'

He smiled at her. 'Then I'd have to teach you how I want it done.'

'So there's nothing I can do.'

'Oh, you can. There's everything to do here.'

Yes, but what she wanted, perhaps arrogantly, was something that only *she* could do, something special. Our magic girl, he had called her once. She was not that any more.

He put down his brush. 'Now you have to go, my dear. I have a meeting of the Housing Group in a few minutes.'

That evening was almost like the days in the Old Work, when they had thrown impromptu parties to celebrate anything out of the ordinary. The God-King's palace had become a barracks for the young soldiers of the new regime – *Leaders* they were called. And now there was no need for concealment – lamps were lit, and music was played – rather dreadful twangy music, Debra thought it, but its gaiety was infectious, and she joined in the clapping and dancing.

There was something, though, that was missing. What was it?

She remembered later on, when one of the Leaders was trying to do a juggling act with beer bottles. He was not very good, and a bottle fell to the marble floor with a crash.

Of course! Palmer!

She wanted to ask someone about the little juggler, but just at that moment, Mara was happily dancing with a fair-haired boy, and none of the others from the Old Work was to be seen.

She asked a freckled boy whose name she did not know, 'What happened to a man called Palmer?' But he merely grinned and shrugged, and she could not tell whether he even understood what she was talking about. Later, someone came in whom she recognised. It was Annet, a shawl wrapped round her head. Annet had

127

grown so thin Debra hardly knew her at first; but there was something familiar in the way she unwound the shawl and almost disdainfully threw the bundle she was carrying onto a table. She looked exhausted, her face waxen, her dark hair dishevelled. She slumped in a chair, and thirstily drank down a flask of beer. Debra did not approach her, not being sure of the reception she would get.

But after a while, Annet seemed to revive. Looking around the room, she saw Debra, and gave a lift of her hand in recognition.

Debra found she was tired too, though the dancing showed no signs of finishing. By London time, it was probably the equivalent of about six o'clock in the morning anyway. Mara had already shown her the bed in the women's dormitory where she was to sleep, so she gathered up her things, took a small oil lamp, and left.

The corridors were silent and spooky in the wavering light of her lamp. She did not like the God-King's palace with its heavy carvings and ugly dark wood – it spoke of tyrants and oppression. You could well imagine that dreadful deeds had been decided inside its massive walls. It was cold too, in spite of the summer outside. She pulled her London coat around her shoulders as she climbed the winding stairway that led to the attic floor where the dormitories were situated.

It was then that she felt something crackling in her pocket. Then she remembered. Of course, it was Matthew's letter. Poor Matthew, she had not given him a thought since she had crossed into the City, and now he seemed so remote, a tiny figure in a distant landscape.

In the big, empty dormitory, she put her lamp down on the little shelf by her bed, and unfolded the letter. In the dim flickering light, Matthew's writing, always untidy and sprawling, was almost unreadable. She had to squint to make the letters come into focus.

Dear Debra,

Well, I'm not much good at writing letters either come to that, but at least I won't make such a cock-up as I did in the park. Not that you were hugely understanding yourself, either, but . . . oh never mind. What I wanted to say, and didn't, was that the time in California was fun, it was fantasy-land, like a dream. I couldn't live like that all the time, I'd go crazy. It wasn't *real*, Debra. Fantasies are fun for a bit, but you can't live in them. Lorri-Anne was nice, she was pretty, she was sexy, all that stuff. She also had a brain about the size of the average flea. I like to be able to hold a conversation. I'm funny that way. So okay, I'm not Einstein, but I'm not a dummy either. The thing I like about you, what I always liked about you, is that you're a real person, I can talk to you. That was why I was mad when you called me thick. So I called you . . . hell, we've been through this one already. Shut your mouth, Best. What the lady wants to hear about is Lorri-Anne, and did the two of you . . . well, yes, as it happens, we did. I'm not made of stone, and it's all a big joke to Lorri-Anne. I'm not exactly proud of it, but I'm not ashamed either. It happened, and it's over, and it isn't important, in spite of what you say, and I don't suppose we'll ever see each other again. Anyway, what about *your* little fling of the Christmas holidays? Don't say you didn't because I know you did. You can't lie to me, girl. So why don't we call it quits, my Lorri-Anne, and your Rhett Butler, whoever he was. We ought to be friends, it's a hell of a waste if we're not.

We don't have to be madly in love, or anything, but I need someone to talk to, and so do you. Neither of us is Miss College Queen 1903, in case you hadn't noticed. Maybe that doesn't sound much of a turn-on, but its *true*. If you and I don't like each other, nobody else will.

I think I've screwed this up too. Oh hell. Anyway, it's late and my brain isn't working. I'll give this to you tomorrow, light the blue touch paper and retire.

Anyway, I'm not going to go chasing you any more. It's up to you. Here's my phone number, at Mum's. Don't be frightened, she won't breathe gin down the line if she answers. Phone me sometime. I hope you will. . . .

Something told her that there was good sense in Matthew's letter. But she could not really concentrate on him and what he was saying. She was in the City now, and the City held her with its own demands.

And in the City, there was unfinished business for her. She did not know yet what it was, but it was niggling at her as she fell asleep.

23

It was still niggling her the following morning when she woke up in the women's dormitory. She found herself alone, everybody already about their duties. The palace was full of people, Leaders, workmen, messengers, and no-one took any notice of her.

Perhaps that was why she felt uncomfortable. Well, that was all right; she wasn't one of those people who needed to be noticed all the time. She would go for a quiet walk by herself; there was still much of the City to get to know.

And she had never got as far as the Poison Tower, though from her window in the Palace she could see its green spindle above the jumbled rooftops.

It should be easy enough to find. She knew it was situated in the Eastern Quarter of the City; and leading off from the square was Eastern Street (or Eesten Street, as she must now think of it) the twin of Southern Street.

Yet Eastern Street was the same as Southern Street and not the same. The same colonnades, the same cobbles, but there was an air of desolation about it, windows shuttered and barred, great green stains of damp running down the stone walls, weeds sprouting from gutters.

The green spire over the rooftops appeared and vanished, appeared and vanished, as she left Eastern

Street, and plunged into the narrow lanes and alleyways of the Eastern Quarter. She saw no-one, and the little houses seemed mostly uninhabited. A coven of wild cats, thin and fierce, stared silently at her from the dark window of a rubble-filled cellar.

The streets wound and twisted so that it was hard to keep the spire in sight. She thought she had lost it, until suddenly, turning a corner, there it was.

It was situated in the centre of a circus of empty buildings. They might have been elegant once, but they were no more, with their flaking stonework, the crumbling patterns of fruit and flowers round windows and arches.

The tower was larger than she had imagined. Placed on a heavy, solid stone base, it rose massively before her, diminishing the grace and slenderness of the spire. A set of narrow steps wound up into the base, to a small door about twelve feet from the ground. The stone wall rose sheerly above that, pierced here and there by tiny windows. As she stared dizzily up, she could just see the curves and curlings of the green spire.

And above the door, tacked roughly to the wall, was one of Cal's famous signs, red paint on brash white.

DAYNJA.
DOO NOT GO IN.

'Mara,' she said later that evening, as the girl was taking her evening meal, 'what happened to Palmer?'

Mara smiled in bewilderment. 'Didn't you know? Palmer died.'

'When did he die?'

'You know. You were here then. It was when you . . .' Suddenly she stopped, and bit her lip. 'Excuse me, I have to go and speak to Jo.' And Mara had gone and for the rest of the evening, she could not be found.

People crowded round her happily that evening. 'Debra, Debra . . .' But she could not concentrate on their chatter. Much later, Annet came in, exhausted as she had been the previous day from her stint at the hospital. She did not seem very approachable, as she sank down on a bench and buried her head in her arms.

'Annet,' Debra said. 'Can we talk?'

Annet raised a face blank with tiredness. 'Now?'

'I wanted to ask you . . .'

Annet sighed, and slowly sat up. She seemed too tired even to protest. She said, 'Seven people died today. There's an outbreak of fever. We couldn't save them. Three were children.'

'I'm sorry,' Debra said. 'Annet, I . . .'

'Well?'

'I have to know what happened to Palmer.'

'He died.'

'I know that.'

'Then why are you asking me?'

'Because there's something you're not telling me.'

'Is there?'

'Yes.'

'What makes you say that?'

'I'm not stupid.'

'Sometimes it's better not to ask questions.'

'What's that supposed to mean?'

Annet sighed. 'I told you to go home, didn't I? You should have listened then.'

In the echoing hall behind them somebody had just started playing one of the monotonous twanging songs on his guitar. Everyone started to join in the words, which were raucous and ribald. The row nearly drowned

Annet's quiet voice. Debra sat down on the bench next to her, and even then had to strain to listen.

'You said I was jealous,' Annet went on. 'Well, perhaps you were right. I used to hero-worship Cal when I was a girl. And you were doing it too.'

'What do you mean?

'Anyone could see that.' Annet cast her a scornful look. 'And he made you feel important; he can be like that when he wants.'

Debra swallowed hard, but she made herself carry on. 'You said you *used* to hero-worship him. What do you mean?'

'Do you really want to hear this?'

'Yes.'

Annet shrugged. 'Of course, I never really knew him that well. By the time I was old enough to remember things, he'd left home. We saw him from time to time. We never knew what he was up to. Well, we know now, of course, and why he couldn't tell us. He was doing wonderful things with prisoners, and people who'd escaped. Nobody else could have done those things. But . . .'

'But what?'

Annet stretched her little hands out in front of her and stared at them. 'We had a dog, a family pet. It had been Cal's when he was a boy, and then it was everyone else's. Cal had adored that dog. We looked after it for him. It wasn't like a dog, it was like a person, we knew it so well. Anyway, it was old, in pain. It had a growth, I think. It was awful for it to be alive like that. When Cal came home, and saw it, he took it outside into the yard. He said, "Come on, here, boy." The dog followed him, of course. It could hardly move but it followed him. Then Cal killed it. He broke its neck with his hands.'

The music became louder and louder. A girl dancing wildly past knocked into Debra and apologised.

Debra said, 'But if the dog was ill . . .'

'It was the best thing for it, only none of us were brave enough. Cal did right, I knew that. But . . .'

'But what?'

'I saw the look on his face after he'd done it. He'd loved that dog, yet he could kill it without a second thought. He didn't mind doing it, that was the point. I thought, then, if he needed me dead, he'd do that too. Without a second thought.'

'What are you trying to tell me?'

'Debra, why do you think they call it the Poison Tower?'

'Something to do with the green colour, Cal said.'

'Because people die, Debra. People die when they go there.'

'But . . .'

'We'd heard stories, of course. People said the Guardians made this poisoned room long long ago because they didn't want anyone finding the books, ever.'

'A poisoned room!'

'So we'd been told.'

'But you didn't know anyone who'd died?'

'We didn't know anyone who'd tried to get in.'

'But you knew there was something?'

'Only one door, with one key! And we got that key. It was too easy. It was too easy for Palmer to get in. Didn't that ever strike you?'

Debra saw that it had not done so at the time. But now it did. One key and an occasional patrol; if the Guardians really cared about making the Tower secure, they could do better than that.

'Did Palmer know it was poisoned?'

'No, of course he wasn't sure, none of us were. The Guardians do plant stories like that to frighten people: this could've been one of them. But he knew it was dangerous, of course. He was scared stiff, to tell you the truth. But he was brave, was Palmer, so he took the risk.'

'What happened?'

'Don't you remember? He was feeling ill when he came back. He knew then. We all did.'

'So . . .?'

'He died. Two days later, I think it was.'

'But that was . . . I was here then . . . nobody . . .'

'No,' Annet said wearily. 'Nobody told you.'

'Why not?'

'Didn't I warn you not to think you belonged?'

'*But why did no-one tell me the room was poisoned?*'

Annet did not answer for a while. Then she said: 'Because Cal ordered us not to, that's why.'

Cal was not in the Palace. He was – well – he had many things to do, many people to see. You couldn't expect it to be just like the old days, opening the ballroom door in the Old Work to find him playing with wooden letters.

So she sat on her bed in the empty dormitory, and said to herself, over and over again, 'I've been a fool. I've been a fool.' But it didn't help.

She found Mara the next day. 'Did *you* know about the Tower? Did Cal tell *you* to keep quiet, too?' In reply, Mara just grinned shamefacedly and wouldn't say anything. Maxon at least had the grace to look troubled when she asked him. 'We felt really bad about it, Debra, really bad.'

'Oh, I'm sure you did.'

'But we needed those books, you see. Cal said we needed them.'

Well, it seemed that however badly the books were needed, nobody had them. They were still hidden in the Poison Tower, and with them, the secret of whatever the City's history had been. Even the Guardians and their puppet God-King, so it seemed, did not know the truth. The skills of reading and writing had been long forgotten, even by them. Cal was mistaken when he imagined otherwise. Apparently, hundreds of years ago, people had been able to put on special suits, like armour, that enabled them to pass through the poisoned room safely, but those suits had long since disintegrated and decayed. Someone was already at work trying to make new ones, but it would take a long time. So there was nothing to stop Cal putting his ugly, logical signs all over the City. There was, after all, no truth, other than what he chose to tell. The history books of the battle were already being written. Debra found a little group at work in one of the many rooms of the Palace. She read: '*Under the rool of the eevel Gardians, menny rongs wer dun to the peepel of the Sity* . . .' They asked for her advice, but laughed when she gave it.

She did not want to help them, anyway. All she wanted was to see Cal.

He came back three days after her conversation with Annet. She did not see him return, but she heard the talk going round that he was there. Everyone wanted to see him about some business or other. It might take days before he had time for her.

Debra did not wait. She ran up the great stairs and along the corridor, her feet echoing on the polished floor. A Leader in trim green uniform, a staff in his hand, a dagger in his belt, stood on guard outside the great double doors of Cal's office. She pushed past him, and through the doors.

'Hey!' the guard cried, 'Stop!'

Cal was sitting at his desk. In front of him, three women were standing. Debra heard him say, 'Very well, we'll have to start distributing from the Northern granary . . .'

He tailed off, in amazement at her intrusion.

'Sorry, sir,' panted the guard. 'She just . . .'

'I have to see you,' said Debra.

He looked at her mildly. 'Debra, I'm busy.'

'I don't care.'

'I have a government to run now. I can't just see people.'

'You can see me. This is important.'

'Come back in an hour's time.'

'*Now!*'

He looked at her for a while. Then he said to the women, 'Very well. I think you've enough there to be getting on with. And you'll have to arrange transport for the potato supplies. Can you do that?'

When the women and the guard had gone, he looked down at his desk for a while. She could see the high pale dome of his forehead. But he did not look angry, when he raised his eyes. He said, 'I can't have people talking to me like that now, Debra.'

'I can't help that,' said Debra.

'Well, say what you have to say. I hope it won't take too long.'

'It won't.'

'I'm listening.'

'It's about the Poison Tower.'

'Well?'

138

'You knew that Palmer was dying. And yet you let me go off too. You knew what would have happened to me if I'd gone in that room. You didn't warn me. You didn't let anyone else warn me.'

He looked across at her, still with the mild half smile on his face.

'Aren't you going to say anything?' Debra said.

'What do you expect me to say? You wouldn't believe me if I denied it.'

'You would have sent me to die!'

'As I remember, it was your idea to go to the Poison Tower. Nobody forced you. You were very eager.'

'Not to die, I wasn't.'

'Palmer was prepared to make the sacrifice. I thought perhaps you might be, too.'

'At least Palmer had the choice. I didn't.'

'You said you'd do anything for us. You said you cared for us.'

'Not to die like that! Without knowing what I was letting myself in for.'

'You wanted to know what you could do for us. Well, I found something you could do.'

'You were just using me.'

'Oh? We saved you from the Guardians, we took you in, we gave you hospitality. How long do you think you would have lasted on the streets without us? Who was using who, Debra?'

'It wasn't like that. You're making it different. You're re-writing it. Just like you're going to do with history. Just like the Guardians did.'

'Our first task was to get rid of the Guardians and what they stood for.'

'And you didn't mind killing people to get there?'

'Some things are more important than people.'

'I don't believe that.'

'You can afford the luxury of thinking so. I can't.'

'But sending me off to . . . I would have died. It was only chance I didn't.'

He riffled through some papers on his desk. 'Very well, you're angry with me. Perhaps you're entitled to be. But now if you'll excuse me, I have things to do.'

'Is that all you've got to say?'

'What else is there? You wouldn't want me to lie to you.'

'I won't just be given the brush-off like that.'

'The brush-off,' he said curiously. 'That must be another of your odd sayings, Debra.'

A few weeks ago, he had kissed her and called her special. Of course it was more than a few weeks for him. It was two years, and you can forget a lot in two years.

But she knew from the way he looked at her that he hadn't forgotten. That wasn't what it was about.

'I trusted you!' she said. 'I trusted you!'

'Did you?' he said, pleasantly smiling up at her. 'Did you? Then you're a fool, Debra. I'm afraid I've never trusted anyone in my life. On the whole, I've found it a good policy. Now you must go. I've given you all the time I can spare.'

24

The Palace was big, it was huge, but when it came to it, it might just as well have been a cardboard box. For there was nowhere to go to be alone. After she had left Cal, she ran straight upstairs to the dormitories. Two girls were sitting there, laughing and mending their green uniforms. On the way downstairs again, she bumped into a group who were setting off for a bread distribution centre; did she want to help? She did not. Some others, laughing and shouting in the corridors, tried to inveigle her to join a working party. The dining hall was taken over by another group who were planning a tour of the Farms.

In the end, she walked the streets. It was a busy market morning, and the main square was filled with stalls and the sound of voices. There was not very much food to be seen on the stalls, a few root vegetables, dried beans, salt fish, but everyone was laughing and happy. Workmen pushed handcarts laden with ladders and pots of paints: all around were sounds of hammering and banging, of a city reconstructing itself. The sun was shining.

She walked aimlessly for the next few hours, and was surprised to find that she had come to the Poison Tower in its circle of silent buildings. Well, at least there was no-one here to bother her. She sat on a step beneath the sign.

It said:

DAYNJA

She wondered if they would ever manage to invent their protective suits, and if so, who would be willing to test them out. Perhaps there would be someone, perhaps not. And if not, the books, whatever they were, would remain untouched, crumbling quietly away. Maybe people would one day burst through the door in perfect safety only to find heaps of dust.

But then, as Cal had said, they didn't really need anyone else's traditions now; they were starting again from scratch. A new world, a new order.

Or was it, or could it be?

It occurred to her that she did not care. Annet was right, she was not part of anything here, only it had taken a betrayal to make her realise that.

And yet she was slow to accept what had happened. She thought, when I go back to the Palace, Cal will be there, looking for me. He will come to meet me, saying Debra, I'm so sorry . . .

For it was a lot to lose all in an instant. If she lost her belief in Cal, then she lost Cal too. If she lost Cal, then she lost the City, the beautiful silent city which had so seduced her with its shadowed streets.

If she lost the City, then that left her with only the things she had before: school, the Orchard Estate, Mum, Shepherd's Bush, Holland Park . . .

Back where she started.

Yet if she returned to the Palace, no doubt there would be a welcome for her. Mara would greet her with a hug, especially if she could believe Debra held no grudge against her. As Maxon had said, they all felt really bad about it. Annet might manage a dry smile. People she did not know would grin and say, 'Hallo, Debra, how's everything going?' Probably even Cal would be nice to her; having forgiven her for today's little outburst he would be prepared to let bygones be bygones, and might even find her a place on a working party, writing textbooks, or helping children to read – just as long as she followed his rules.

She could stay here forever, no doubt about that.

But the thing was, and she saw it now, and as she saw it, realised that part of her had always known it underneath, nobody here was really interested in her. She had come magically to them out of a different world, bearing bus tickets and labelled sweaters, and had shown them how to write their names. And they'd misunderstood even that, most of them thinking that what she offered was some sort of lucky charm. It could have been anybody who came to them out of the blue, and they would have given that anybody the same enthusiastic reception. What she was, what she, Debra Stoner, *really* was, was of very little interest to them.

And she saw now that it mattered to her that people know her for what she was. All her life she'd resented the life she was born into, she'd resented the Orchard Estate, the clamour and the ugliness and the mess of it. Sometimes, as she watched the wealthy families who lived near the school piling into their Volvos, going off to their houses in the country, their ponies and possessions, she had felt that she was doomed to live a kind of half-life, in her thirteenth floor flat, without a father, and with a mother who was too exhausted from her job in Tesco's to do anything most evenings other than collapse in front of television and a frozen meal. She'd resented the fact that at school, it seemed to be always the other girls who had the boys rushing round like bees round a flower, the other girls who could walk elegantly down the corridors, slim, spotless, and wearing the kind of clothes you saw in magazines. She had felt that when the worldly and spiritual goods were being dished out, she, Debra Stoner, had come off an extremely poor second.

But the slim blonde girls in the Volvos might end up in finishing schools, simply arranging the flowers and setting tables for dinner parties; lovely Rachel Ward might be pushing two toddlers disconsolately round in a pram in a few years' time. You couldn't choose some bits and discard others. What she was, for good or ill, had been made by life on the Orchard Estate, by having to use her brain and her wits, never being able to rely on her looks to get her anything, or the fact that Daddy had the right contacts. She didn't *want* to be anyone else when it came to the point.

Of course, there was, if she wanted it, a new life waiting for her in the City, among all the bright-eyed, enthusiastic people busily engaged on pulling a society to pieces and rebuilding it in their own image.

Well, good luck to them. She hoped they'd succeed.

It just wasn't for her, that's all.

The sun had gone in, and the colours were fading. Perhaps it would soon be dark in the City. She pulled her coat around her, and as she did so, could feel Matthew's letter in her pocket. It would be nice to have him as a friend. Were they the soul-mates he had suggested in his letter? Well, perhaps they were, perhaps they weren't. Only time would tell. And the process of finding out might be interesting.

There was something else in her pocket too. A felt-tip pen. She thought, if only that had just happened to be among the furniture of her coat the last time she'd come to the City, what a lot of trouble it would have saved them, all the looking for chalk and charcoal and paint.

That simple pen would have made all the difference.

But in the end it wouldn't have mattered. In the end, there would still have been Cal and his signs, written the way he wanted them to be, using whatever, and whoever, he could find.

It was growing darker now, and the City was still. The streets were swallowed up in the darkness, everything was one-dimensional, like an old film-set, where the buildings were simply flats that would fall down if you touched them.

For some reason, a scene came to her mind from a book she had read years ago now, and only half-recalled. It was Alice, preparing to leave her Looking-Glass world as everything collapsed around her. She remembered what Alice had called out scornfully as she prepared to return home, and the words went round and round in her brain.

Around her, the City grew dim and insubstantial. Would there be a door back? There had always been a door before, even sometimes when she had not wanted it. She would find her way back.

But there was something else to do first. She took the pen out of her pocket, and went up to the little door of the Poison Tower. It was painted a nice matt green and stood out, even in the gloom. Well, only one person in the City would be able to read her message, and even he would not understand the reference. Perhaps one day, he'd be one of the people who would enter the Poison Tower, and among the strange archives, the telephone directories and goodness knows what, he'd find that particular classic, and come across her reference.

Even then he probably wouldn't have the faintest idea what she was getting at. Wouldn't even care, most likely. But she did not intend to leave the City without making this tiny mark on its fabric.

She wrote:

YOU'RE NOTHING BUT A PACK OF CARDS.

It was so dark now that she could barely see the buildings around her; only a dense twilight.

She began to walk briskly away from the Poison Tower, and even her own footsteps sounded insubstantial on the cobbles, as though there was cotton wool on the ground. Shapes loomed up and filled the spaces around her, walls, buildings she did not recognise.

And now she began to break into a run, through the dark streets. There was not a light to guide her, not a sound. Everywhere the dense stillness of fog. Only at the edges of her vision the flick-flick-flick of walls, as she pulled away from them, left them behind her. The City unrolled like a dark tunnel before her, and closed up behind her; she ran and ran without knowing where she went. Eesten Street, Suthen Street, the Palace, the ruined Old Work, the empty fountains, the crumbled pillars, the bronzed, ornate stone, all was behind her now. All she thought about was the running, and the tug of breath in her chest, the rhythms of her feet.

So dark, so foggy. No night was ever like this.

And yet she felt now that she was through it; and here and there, just out of the corner of her eye, glimpsed for a second, and then swallowed up, came the flash of lights, silver, red, green.

Walls sheered off around her, great soundless cliffs rearing up before her and settling themselves around her as she passed. Noises came through the silence like foghorns booming through a dark sea, a roaring that soon became a rattling and a rumble. The scale of everything had opened up, as a cinema screen unfolds in the darkness, there were great buildings around her, wide streets, tall towers. The flashing lights now strung themselves together in streaks of neon green, crimson, reflecting from plate glass windows and on wet black streets. She heard people laughing, shouting, and she slowed down. The vivid lemon yellow lights of a Macdonalds shone out, and in front of her, a girl was saying to her boyfriend, 'Elmers End! I ask you! She expects me to go to Elmers End!' She stopped, gasping for breath. 'Chipboard with a walnut veneer,' said one man to another, 'or you could have a teak, I suppose.' 'Underneath the bureau drawer, just where I told you,' a woman admonished her husband. 'Friday week,' said a girl. 'You'd better.' Debra wanted to hug her, and reached out to touch her. The girl saw, and looked startled. 'Sorry,' said Debra. The girl shrugged and walked off. A bus trundled by at her shoulder. It was a 27. The 27 was famous for never being visible, but here was one. A huge lorry. Cars. Motorcyclists.

Somewhere in a high room, a man dressed in dark clothes sat awkwardly writing, dusty sunlight coming through the windows, an image in a dream that would neither fade away nor come closer.

Somewhere.

There was a telephone kiosk on the corner. A man came out of it, so it must be working. She reached in her pocket for Matthew's letter, and found, too, a handful of coins. She went into the kiosk, and began, slowly, to press out the code of Matthew's phone number.

Tony Drake

NO TIME TO SAY GOODBYE

Martin was bowled over by Cath. Imagine an attractive, smart, well-heeled girl like her being interested in him. And everything was so easy with her – Cath led and Martin just followed. He liked her a lot, even though he didn't always approve of the things she got up to.

Martin didn't even mind about Cath's friend Gee, who always seemed to be around. He had heard rumours about the sort of business Gee was mixed up in, but he was fun, he knew how to have a good time. One thing was for sure, Martin's life was more exciting for knowing Cath and Gee. The trouble was, he didn't know what their game was – until he was in it up to his neck . . .

Anthony Masters

ALL THE FUN OF THE FAIR

Jim North and his Gallopers – a beautifully painted and carved fairground ride – have an annual date at the Starling Point estate. But this year they have not bargained for the dramatic end of Gerry Kitson's mystery ride, nor the arrival of their new assistant, Leroy. And as Leroy desperately tries to prove himself, the battle to save the Gallopers, not only from bankruptcy but also from vandalism, begins.

ALL THE FUN OF THE FAIR is the first in the *Starling Point* series. Other titles available are:

CAT BURGLARS
SIEGE
AFRICAN QUEEN

Jenny Nimmo

THE SNOW SPIDER

"Time to find out if you are a magician!" said Gwyn's grandmother, as she gave him five strange birthday gifts. What could they mean? The piece of seaweed, the yellow scarf, the tin whistle, the twisted metal brooch and the small broken horse? Gwyn gave the brooch to the wind and, in return, there came a tiny silver spider, Arianwen. The snow spider.

So begins an extraordinary account of battles against evil and encounters with other worlds of snow and silver.

EMLYN'S MOON

"Don't go into Llewelyn's chapel! No good will come of it. Something happened there!" But if Nia hadn't gone in, her life would never have changed so.

The second book in THE SNOW SPIDER trilogy.

THE CHESTNUT SOLDIER

For three years Gwyn has not grown, and his magic powers have become a burden to him. Then Evan Llyr, a soldier seeks refuge in the village, and Gwyn has new conflicts to resolve. Gwyn feels a strange affinity with the soldier, but as autumn burns into the mountain, he knows he must do battle with him – a battle in which one of them will perish.

The Chestnut Soldier triumphantly concludes the trilogy begun with *The Snow Spider* and continued by *Emlyn's Moon*. It is an astonishing, beautiful story of the triumph of love and loyalty over hatred and evil.

Gillian Rubinstein

BEYOND THE LABYRINTH

Growing up seems difficult enough for Brenton. He can't get on with his parents, his youngest brother is taller than he is and seems to be overtaking him in every way, and his mother has invited 12-year-old Victoria Hare to stay while her parents are overseas. But in comparison with personal problems, the threat of nuclear annihilation is so overwhelming that Brenton no longer wishes to take responsibility for his actions, preferring to act upon the throw of the dice. Life becomes more complicated when an alien anthropologist arrives to study an ancient Aboriginal tribe who once lived in the area around his home – does she confirm his worst fears?

Diana Wynne Jones

HOMEWARD BOUNDERS

Jamie liked exploring and he wasn't above trespassing. But shut in the eerie silence of the strange little park – right in the centre of the noisy city – Jamie knew he should never have climbed over the wall. Jamie's curiosity leads him farther away than he ever imagined – into strange and unknown worlds where anything might happen and where he becomes a pawn in a terrifying game of survival.

Gillian Rubinstein

SPACE DEMONS

Space Demons is a computer game with a difference. Imported directly from Japan, it's a prototype destined to lock four unlikely individuals into deadly combat with the sinister forces of its intelligence.

And, as the game draws them into its powerful ambit, Andrew Hayford, Elaine Taylor, Ben Challis and Mario Ferrone are also forced to confront the darker sides of their own natures.

"A wonderful book . . . there's so much to enjoy and reflect on." *Books for Keeps*

Honour Award Australian Book of the Year
Peace Award for Children's Literature
Winner 1988 South Australian Festival Awards

Margaret Mahy

THE HAUNTING

"When, suddenly, on an ordinary Wednesday, it seemed to Barney that the world tilted and ran downhill in all directions, he knew he was about to be haunted again."

Tabitha can't help noticing the change in Barney – how quiet he's become, his pale expression and those dazed eyes which seem to be seeing things from another world. But as Tabitha determines to solve the mystery she finds herself in very deep waters. Who was Barney's Great-Uncle Cole? Is he really dead? And who can save Barney from the terrifying experiences which seem to be taking hold of him?

"Strong and terrifying . . . The novel winds up like a spring. A psychological thriller."

Times Literary Supplement

Diana Wynne Jones

FIRE AND HEMLOCK

Suddenly Polly begins to remember . . .

Halloween, nine years ago. She gatecrashed a funeral party at the big house. She met Tom Lynn for the first time. And he gave her the strange photograph of the hemlock flowers and the fire.

But what has happened in the years between? Why has Polly erased Tom from her own mind and the rest of the world as well? How could she have forgotten him when he had meant so much to her? And how can she unlock her memory, before her quest becomes a matter of life or death . . .

A fascinating story of intrigue and sorcery.

A Selected List of Fiction from Mammoth

While every effort is made to keep prices low, it is sometimes necessary to increase prices at short notice. Mammoth Books reserves the right to show new retail prices on covers which may differ from those previously advertised in the text or elsewhere.

The prices shown below were correct at the time of going to press.

☐	416 13972 8	**Why the Whales Came**	Michael Morpurgo	£2.50
☐	7497 0034 3	**My Friend Walter**	Michael Morpurgo	£2.50
☐	7497 0035 1	**The Animals of Farthing Wood**	Colin Dann	£2.99
☐	7497 0136 6	**I Am David**	Anne Holm	£2.50
☐	7497 0139 0	**Snow Spider**	Jenny Nimmo	£2.50
☐	7497 0140 4	**Emlyn's Moon**	Jenny Nimmo	£2.25
☐	7497 0344 X	**The Haunting**	Margaret Mahy	£2.25
☐	416 96850 3	**Catalogue of the Universe**	Margaret Mahy	£1.95
☐	7497 0051 3	**My Friend Flicka**	Mary O'Hara	£2.99
☐	7497 0079 3	**Thunderhead**	Mary O'Hara	£2.99
☐	7497 0219 2	**Green Grass of Wyoming**	Mary O'Hara	£2.99
☐	416 13722 9	**Rival Games**	Michael Hardcastle	£1.99
☐	416 13212 X	**Mascot**	Michael Hardcastle	£1.99
☐	7497 0126 9	**Half a Team**	Michael Hardcastle	£1.99
☐	416 08812 0	**The Whipping Boy**	Sid Fleischman	£1.99
☐	7497 0033 5	**The Lives of Christopher Chant**	Diana Wynne-Jones	£2.50
☐	7497 0164 1	**A Visit to Folly Castle**	Nina Beachcroft	£2.25

All these books are available at your bookshop or newsagent, or can be ordered direct from the publisher. Just tick the titles you want and fill in the form below.

Mandarin Paperbacks, Cash Sales Department, PO Box 11, Falmouth, Cornwall TR10 9EN.

Please send cheque or postal order, no currency, for purchase price quoted and allow the following for postage and packing:

UK   80p for the first book, 20p for each additional book ordered to a maximum charge of £2.00.

BFPO   80p for the first book, 20p for each additional book.

Overseas   £1.50 for the first book, £1.00 for the second and 30p for each additional book
including Eire thereafter.

NAME (Block letters) ....MAREE Hume...........................

ADDRESS .....40....woodhead..st.................................

..........High...valley...field...........................

.....fife.......ky12 5SQ...........................